TRIBUTE
TO
TAGORE

Yasmin Faruque

Order this book online at www.trafford.com
or email orders@trafford.com

Most Trafford titles are also available at major online book retailers.

Printed in the United States of America.

ISBN: 978-1-4669-4756-6 (sc)
ISBN: 978-1-4669-4757-3 (e)

Trafford rev. 07/23/2012

 www.trafford.com

North America & international
toll-free: 1 888 232 4444 (USA & Canada)
phone: 250 383 6864 ♦ fax: 812 355 4082

CONTENTS

DEDICATION

To the person who infused my life
With significance,
Who reciprocated all the love I gave him
With twice as much
My sweet son Shams

PREFACE

R ABINDRANATH TAGORE IS the life-force of Bangla literature. His contributions to the cultural life of West Bengal and Bangladesh are beyond measure. In fact there is no area of Bangla literature that he did not touch. He composed more than 1,000 songs including the national anthems of both India and Bangladesh, numerous dances such as **Shyama**, **Chandalika,** plays such as **Raja**, **Raktakaravi**, 200+ short stories like **Drishtidaan**, **Kabuliwala**, many essays &letters and last but not least, a dozen witty, pithy and insightful novels such as **Naukadubi, Bou Thakuranir Haat,** in addition to numerous volumes of poetry, exploring a number of issues.

I pay my tribute to Tagore with translations of some of his beautiful stories. I hope my tiny effort pleases my readers, and that they forgive any mistakes that I may have made inadvertently.

Yasmin Faruque
Grand Forks, North Dakota
July 8, 2012

BIOGRAPHY OF TAGORE

RABINDRANATH TAGORE, WHO infused new life into the nearly stagnant Bangla literature, was born at Tagore House, Jorasanko, Kolkata, the ancestral family home, on May 11, 1861. Neither his father, Maharshi Debendranath Tagore, nor his mother, Sarada Devi, had any inkling that their youngest child would grow up to be such an icon in the field of Bangla Literature. Being the youngest of fifteen, young Rabindranath had a posse of caretakers.

Rabindranath was sent to boarding school when he was nine years old. However, the strict rules there did not agree with his sensitive nature, and he came home at thirteen, never to return there. Afterwards, a virtual contingent of house tutors took care of his schooling.

Many of Tagore's siblings were poets and songwriters in their own right. Seeing them, Tagore was also inspired to write. His tutors also helped in this regard.

At seventeen, Tagore was sent to England to study law. But whoever heard of a poet being shackled by legal jargon? His study of law did not come to fruition. Returning home, the young poet had his first book of poems, Bonophul, published. Other books, Kori O Komal, Shishu Bholanath, Probhat Sangeet, Sandhya Sangeet, Manoshi, Shonaar Tori, Chitra followed in rapid succession.

At twenty-two, Tagore married eighteen-year-old Mrinalini Devi of South Dihi, Khulna. Together, the couple raised three daughters, Madhurilata (Bela), Mira and Renuka (Rani), & two sons, Rathindranath and Shamindranath.

For his contributions to literature, Tagore received the Nobel Prize for Literature in 1913. His beautiful songbook, Gitanjali, played a significant part in this.

In 1915, Tagore was knighted by the British King. However, in 1919, in response to the atrocities by the British army in Jalianwalabagh that killed so many, he flung it away like a discarded garment.

After having received the Nobel Prize, Tagore turned his attention to prose for a time. It was during this time that he penned twelve witty, pithy, insightful novels and the beautiful short stories contained in the volume Golpoguccho or A Bunch of Stories. These stories speak of ordinary events that became extraordinary, shining out like beacons by Tagore's exquisite golden touch.

Tagore passed away on August 7, 1941. He was mourned by myriads of mourners worldwide. During the War of Liberation for Bangladesh in 1971, Tagore's writings proved inspiring; Bangladesh adopted his beautiful patriotic song Amar shonaar Bangla Ami Tomay Bhalobashi (My Golden Bangla, how I do adore thee!) as her national anthem after liberation. The national anthem of India is also from his roster of songs. Although he is no more, his writings will continue to inspire.

1 A TALE OF TWO FATHERS (ORIGINAL: KABULIWALA)

A father's love is as sweet as nectar, as nourishing as ambrosia. It has borne through the ages, transcending all cultures, races and creeds. In the story, A Tale of Two Fathers, Tagore has written of the love that a Bengali father has for his little girl. This love is echoed by the affections of the Kabuliwala, an Afghan fruit-vendor, for the same little lady. In this beautiful story, Tagore has portrayed this feelingly.

MY DAUGHTER MINI, a little damsel just turned five years old, finds it very hard indeed not to talk. After birth, she took less than a year to learn to talk; from then on, nearly all her waking moments have been spent talking. She wastes no time being silent. Her mother sometimes scolds her into silence, but to me a silent Mini looks so unnatural that I can never bring myself to do that; so with me she talks spiritedly.

That morning I had just begun Chapter Seventeen of the novel I was working on when Mini came in and began right away, "Papa, the doorman Ramdayal calls crows black birds. Boy, how stupid he is!"

Before I could explain to her the various ways to express oneself, she hurriedly changed the subject, "See, Papa, Bhola says it rains because elephants squirt the sky with water that they spray with their trunks. Oh, Bhola talks such nonsense, day and night!"

Not waiting for my opinion on this, she continued, asking abruptly, "Papa dear, what is Mama to you?"

To myself I smiled and said, "Sister-in-law." To her I said aloud, "Mini darling, why don't you go play with Bhola? I have work to do now."

She then sat down at the foot of my little writing table and began playing a rhyming game with her hands and knees, repeating herself faster and faster every time. In my Chapter Seventeen the hero & the heroine were just then about to jump from a third-story prison window onto the swirling river below on a pitch-dark cloudy night.

My study faces the road; suddenly leaving off her game, Mini ran to the open window and called loudly, "Kabuliwala, hey Kabuliwala!"

A tall Kabuliwala, with peach-fair skin tanned brown by the Calcutta sun, dressed in loose, none-too-clean looking clothes and with a turban on his head, was sauntering slowly by; he had a cloth bag slung across one shoulder and a few boxes of dried fruit and nuts in his hands. It is difficult to say what my precious daughter thought upon seeing him, but I could not stop her from calling loudly out to him. I thought, "Oh, no! Here comes a living nuisance, bag on shoulder and everything. Now I can never finish my Chapter XVII."

However, no sooner had the Kabuliwala turned towards our house with a smile on Mini's call and begun to come forth than Mini turned on her heels and ran indoors so fast that she was hardly more than a streak. She was convinced that had she looked inside that bag, she would have found a few children just like her.

Meanwhile the Kabuliwala had come right in and paid his respects with a smile. While my hero and heroine were in dire peril, I thought, it is very rude to call him here and then not buy anything. I bought a little something, and then conversed on sundry topics. At last, getting up to go, he asked in a booming but gentle voice, "Babuji, where is your little girl?"

To break Mini's irrational fear I called her out; she came with hesitant steps and then stayed close by me, casting dubious glances at the Kabuli's face and sack. When the Kabuli offered her a treat of fruit and nuts from his bag, she would not accept it, and clung apprehensively to my knees. So passed the first meeting.

Some days later, I needed to come out of the house to go somewhere. Beside the front door I saw my baby sitting on the bench, talking nonstop to the same Kabuliwala; he was at her feet, listening intently and in appropriate places offering his opinion in Bengali so broken up and mixed with his native Pashtu it sounded like gibberish. In all her five years my little Mini had never had a listener as avid as this, except of course for me. I noticed again her little scarf full of nuts and dried fruit. I said to the Kabuliwala, "What is this? Please don't give her things like this anymore." Taking a half-rupee coin from my pocket, I held it out to him. Without hesitation he took it and put it in his bag.

On returning home I found that very little coin the center of a heated, sometimes tearful argument between Mini and her mother; Mini's mother, holding out a shiny, round silver piece, was asking, "Where did you get this coin?"

"The Kabuliwala gave it me," Mini was replying.

"But why ever would you take it from him?" Again came the question.

About to burst into floods of tears, Mini said, "I didn't want it. He gave it me himself."

I was informed that this was not the second meeting between these two; the Kabuli came nearly every day, and by bribing Mini with fruit and nuts, had taken over her little enticed heart almost entirely.

I noticed that these two friends, one so much older than the other, had a few standard jokes—such as when she saw Rahmat Mini would ask laughingly, "Kabuliwala, O Kabuliwala, what's that inside your sack?"

With a smile the Kabuliwala would reply nasally, "An elephant." That a huge elephant could fit inside that fairly small sack of his was the punch line of the joke. It wasn't that witty, but the two friends enjoyed it a whole lot—and their pleasure, shining out like the golden autumn sunlight in laughter simple and sweet, made me happy too.

There was another standard joke between them. Rahmat would ask Mini, "Baby mine, won't you ever go to your in-laws' place?"

Now, a Bengali girl grows up with some idea of what her in-laws' place should be like. However, we being ultramodern hadn't really explained this to our baby girl. So it happened that she wouldn't really understand the question. Yet not to reply was also against her grain—so she would fire back, "Would you?"

Lifting a huge fist towards an imaginary father-in-law, Rahmat would say, "I will hit the father-in-law."

Hearing this and picturing the sad plight of the unfamiliar father-in-law, Mini would break into peals of amused laughter.

Autumn has arrived, nut-brown overlaid with gold. In days of yore, this was the time when Kings and emperors would set out on conquests. Now, I have never left my little home here in an obscure corner of Calcutta—but my unfettered mind roams freely all over everywhere. It's as if I've been forever doomed to stay home, so my heart yearns for foreign lands. A foreigner whom I meet perchance may bring a picture of a mountain retreat to mind and the desire to be free to go anywhere overtakes me, bringing with it a desire for the freedom to live as I please.

Then again, I happen to be so introverted that the very notion of leaving my little sheltered nook makes my world fall apart. As such these morning conversations with this big Kabuli sufficed for a bit of travel. I imagined myself traveling with a herd of camels through narrow serpentine passes between towering, almost impassable mountain ranges. Pedestrians and camel-riders carrying lances and flint-locks appeared in my mind's eye as the Kabuli, in Bengali very broken up indeed and in a voice like thunder, talked of the homeland he had left behind.

Now, Mini's mother is a very apprehensive person. When she hears a noise out on the street, she fears all the alcoholics of the town targeting our home for an attack. She pictures this world as being overrun with thieves, robbers, alcoholics, poisonous snakes, man-eating tigers, malaria, caterpillars, big red-brown cockroaches and the British ruling class; in her fairly short stay in this world, this opinion has not changed.

She wasn't totally easy about Rahmat Kabuliwala. She repeatedly requested me to keep a close eye on him. When I tried to laugh her fears away, she asked me a few pointed questions:

"Were children never kidnapped? Is slavery not practiced in Kabul? Would it be so very impossible for a huge Kabuli to steal away a small child?"

I had to agree that kidnapping, while not impossible, would be improbable. The power to believe is not equally bestowed on everyone, so my wife retained her doubts. However, while Rahmat was totally innocent of having offended, I could not turn him away from our door.

Every year, Rahmat would go home at the end of January. He is very busy then, collecting his year's dues. Even though he had to go door to door, he would still come to see Mini once a day. When he couldn't come in the morning, he appeared in the evening. To see them talking there together, one would think they were hatching naughty plots. To tell the truth, the sight of the big shabbily-clad fellow sitting in a dark corner of my front room at dusk made me a little afraid, too; but when I saw my tiny Mini come calling out to him, and the old pat jokes go on, I was happy.

One morning I sat in my small front room reading galley-proofs. The last two days had turned bitter cold, for Father Winter, before his final goodbye, was hugging our city tight. The warm glow of the morning sunlight, coming in through the east window and falling on my feet under the table, made them feel warm and toasty. It was around eight then, and almost all the wrapped- up morning- walkers had returned home. Meanwhile, a great hue and cry came from the road in front of our house.

Looking out, I saw our Rahmat, handcuffed and chained, being led by two guardsmen towards the police-station—followed by a long line of curious neighborhood children. The front of Rahmat's shirt was bloodstained, and one of the guardsmen held a saber still dripping blood. Going out on my verandah, I asked one guardsman what had gone on.

I learned partly from him, partly from Rahmat, that a neighbor of ours owed Rahmat the price of a Rampuri woolen shawl. When he had falsely denied that claim, a fight had broken out, in the course of which Rahmat had stabbed him.

Rahmat was heaping abuses on the liar when Mini came dancing out, calling, "Kabuliwala, hey Kabuliwala!"

Rahmat's gloomy face lit up at once in a sunny smile. He had no bag on his shoulder today, so their usual chatter about it was passed by. Mini asked right out, "Would you go to your in-laws' place?"

"That's where I'm off to now," said Rahmat. Seeing that Mini didn't even smile, he held up his hands and said, "I would like to hit the father-in-law, but how can I when my hands are tied?'

Rahmat was given eight years for causing serious bodily harm to a person.

We nearly put him out of mind. While we sat at home carrying on with our daily life, a fiercely independent Rahmat was doing time in prison. No doubt it was gut-wrenching, but we did not let it bother us much.

Moreover, my fickle Mini had shamelessly forgotten her old comrade, and first made friends with Nabi the stable groom. Then, as she grew older, the number of her girl-friends went up. She has even stopped coming out to my study. I've not spoken to her heart to heart for quite a while.

The years slipped by like pearls being strung. Another golden autumn spread her sheen over our city. A bridegroom had been found for my Mini; she, the joyous laughter of my home, was to be married during the Puja holidays, and go to her in-laws' place with the immersion of the Mother-goddess.

The morning had dawned especially beautiful. After the incessant downpours of the Rains, the early autumn sunshine seemed like pure molten gold. Even the congested homes of my Calcutta neighborhood seemed overlaid with a special comeliness.

Ere morning had dawned, the oboe started playing at my house. The sad but sweet notes wrenched my heart with tears of separation and sadness. The plaintive notes of the early morning raga Bhairavi spread the sadness of my imminent separation in all directions. Today is my sweet Mini's wedding-day.

From early morning, there was hustle and bustle everywhere, with people coming and going about various tasks. The bamboo platform for the canopy was being set up; in every room of the house as well as out on the verandah, chandeliers and strings of colored lights were going up with tinkles and rings; it was very busy and noisy.

I was in my reading-room, updating my account-book, when Rahmat came in and salaamed.

At first I found it difficult to recognize him. He had no bag, his long hair was replaced by an army cut, and he seemed weak & a little out-of-sorts; at last his smile gave him away.

"Why, if it isn't Rahmat! When didst thou come back?" I asked, as heartily as I could.

"I was released from prison last evening," he replied.

Those words jarred my ears; I'd never before laid eyes on a killer, so the sight of this one made my heart squeeze small; I wished for this man to get out of here on this auspicious day.

I said, "There is something going on at home today; I am rather busy, so please go."

Hearing this he turned to go at once, but at the door he hesitated, asking, "Please can't I see my darling Baby just once?"

He must have clung to the hope that Mini was just like before, and would come out calling to him. There would still be the same old jokes, over which they would laugh heartily. He had even borrowed boxes of dried fruit and nuts from a compatriot of his, remembering the close friendship of days gone by, because his own bag was no more.

I said to him, "We are very busy at home today; thou canst not meet anyone."

He was hurt and upset. Standing very still he looked me steadily in the eye and then, saying, "Babu, Salaam," went out the door.

I felt a pang of pain; I was just about to call out after him when he returned of his own accord.

Coming near he pressed the boxes into my hand, "I brought these boxes of nuts and fruit for my Baby. Please see that she gets them."

Taking them, I was just about to pay him when he grasped my tiny hand in his huge fist, "You are so kind. I'll always remember you.—Please don't try to pay me.—Babu, I too have a daughter like yours, at home. It is her face that brings me to see Baby; I don't come here on business."

So saying he put his hand inside his loose garments and from near the breast brought out a small piece of dirty paper, unfolding it with care and spreading it out in front of me.

I saw that on the paper was the print of a tiny hand. It was no photograph or oil-painting, just the print of a small hand dipped in soot and held onto the paper. With this bit of memento of his baby girl next to his breast sweetening his exile Rahmat hawks fruit and nuts year after year on the Calcutta roads.

This little paper brought tears to my own eyes; I forgot then that he was a Kabuli fruit-vendor and I a respectable Bengali gentleman. He is what I am, I thought, we are both fathers. The memento of his little girl waiting for him in her mountain retreat brought my own Mini to mind, and I called her out. The women indoors objected vehemently, but I did never listen. Mini, dressed in her bridal finery and made up, came and stood bashfully by me.

Rahmat was taken aback on seeing her like this; not for worlds now would he begin on their old jokes. With a laugh he asked at last, "Baby mine, would you go to your in-laws' place?"

Mini, who understood now the meaning of in-laws' place, blushed red and turned away without answering. My mind flashed back to the day when Rahmat and Mini had first met and I felt a lump rising in my throat.

When Mini had gone back indoors, Rahmat sat down hard on the floor with a deep sigh. He realized clearly now that his little girl too must have grown up in all these years, and that he would probably have to get to know her all over again. Who knows what happened to her in all these years? The oboe kept on playing in the soft autumn morning light, and Rahmat, sitting in a Calcutta lane, dreamed of his mountain home in Afghanistan.

I handed him a hundred-rupee bill, saying, "Rahmat my friend, go back home to your daughter. May your meeting bless my darling Mini."

Giving away this bill meant I had to curtail an aspect or two of the festivities. I could not have as many electric lights as I'd wanted, nor did the band come to play. The ladies indoors were quite displeased, but the benevolent glow of a father's love shed over my auspicious feast a radiance unequalled.

2 DASHED DESIRES
(ORIGINAL: DURASHAA)

This story, although it is a figment of the imagination, underlines a truth. Humanity is above race, caste and creed. Nobody deserves to be tortured, least of all a woman.

ARRIVING AT DARJEELING, I found the weather very inclement indeed. I wouldn't want to go out then, but to stay in was not it, to go out would be even worse. After breakfast in the hotel diner, I donned my McIntosh and thick rain boots, and ventured out for a short stroll. It was drizzling on and off, and there was such thick cloud-cover that it seemed God Almighty Himself had taken a monstrous eraser and tried to rub out the entire landscape, including the Himalayas, and had succeeded beyond belief.

I was sauntering by mine own lonely self on the desolate Calcutta Road, thinking that this cloud-realm with nothing to hold onto doesn't appeal to me any more—I want to hug this mother earth, with all her wealth of sound, touch and beauty, in my five fingers, whatever it takes.

In the meantime I heard the sound of a woman weeping, not very far off. In this temporal life, full of the slings and arrows of outrageous fortune as it is, the sound of weeping is not so strange. I doubt if I would even look back at any other place or time, but under this unbelievably thick cloud-cover, that sound caught me as being the only one in a world deep in slumber, not to sneeze at.

Following the sound, I ventured nearer and found a saffron-clad woman, with her tangled golden-brown tresses piled atop her head in a loose topknot, sitting on a stone by the wayside weeping her heart out. This was not the lament of a recent grief. Rather, it was the outpouring of a pent-up sense of weary suffering, kept quiet for a very long time. It broke forth now, like a river overflowing her banks, on this inclement day.

O, this is great, I thought, it begins just like a made-up tale. I hadn't even had inkling that I would someday meet an ascetic woman sitting on a mountaintop weeping as hard as this.

I couldn't tell what ethnic group the woman was of. I asked kindly in Hindi, "Who are you, my dear? What's the matter with you?"

At first she answered me not, looking at me with burning tearful eyes. I said once more,

"Fear me not, my dear. I'm a gentleman, I am."

Hearing this she laughed and said in the most perfect Hindi, "I gave up being afraid long ago. I have no modesty either. Babuji, the zenana where I once lived was off limits even to my own little brother. Today, here I am, sitting out in the open for the whole world to see."

At first I was a little miffed. In my attire and conduct I am wholly European. But then what made this poor woman address me as Babuji, so unhesitatingly? No more indeed, I thought, I should end this novel of mine right here and now and depart, smoking all the way like a train thumbing its nose at everything, noisily, fast and with bravado. But at last my curiosity did kill the cat, and I asked, "Do you need anything? Can I be of any help?"

She looked me steadily in the eye, and a little later answered tersely, "I am the daughter of Nawab Ghulam Quadir Khan of Badraon."

Where on earth Badraon is, who Nawab Ghulam Quadir Khan happens to be, or what sort of dire predicament would lead his daughter to choose this particular stretch of road to let loose her pent-up grief, I had no need to know and indeed never believed. However, I had no inclination to intrude; the story was just beginning to get interesting.

Right then and there, I assumed a grave face and salaamed, "I beg your pardon, Your Ladyship. I didn't recognize you."

There were many logical reasons behind my not recognizing her. Firstly, I'd never laid eyes upon her before. Secondly, in this miserably dark and foggy weather, I'd have had difficulty discerning mine own hands and feet.

My Lady took no offence and, pointing to a nearby stone, commanded in a contented tone,

"Please do take a seat."

I saw that this woman had the capacity to command. I felt myself blest in a certain way at having received that permission to sit near her on that mossy stone slab. The daughter of Nawab Ghulam Quadir Khan of Badraon, the Princess Mihr-un-Nisa'a or Nur-un-Nisa'a or mayhaps even Nur-ul-Mulk, had granted me leave to sit next her on that slippery, moss-covered stone. When I'd ventured forth from the hotel in my McIntosh and boots, this great opportunity hadn't even dawned on me.

On the lap of the Himalayas, a man and a woman sitting close together in conversation seem as sweet and warm as a poem just concluded, giving rise in the readers' hearts of the sound of a fountain unleashed from a faraway, lonely mountaintop cave and awakening the musical murmur of the Kumarasambhava and the Meghaduta, both by the poet Kalidasa. Even so, one has to own up that upstarts brash enough to sit in conversation with Princesses on mossy stones by the side of Calcutta Road in weather as bad as this, and feel proud, are few and far between. However, that particular day was so gloomy under thick cloud-cover that there was no need to be reticent or embarrassed—only in that kingdom of cloud-shadows were the daughter of Nawab Ghulam Quadir Khan of Badraon and I, a newly-risen Bengali Sahib, sitting there on our two stone slabs like two remnants of the annihilation of the world; none but our Fate saw this farce of a meeting between us.

I asked, "Bibi Sahib, who did this to you?"

Striking her forehead with her open palm, the Princess of Badraon said, "How do I know Who makes these things happen? Who has enveloped these towering, tough, rocky Himalayas in an insignificant fleecy mantle of clouds?"

Without philosophizing, I concurred in everything, "That's so. Who can decipher the mysteries of Fate? We are but as insignificant as small insects."

I'd have raised arguments, not letting the Bibi Sahib off the hook so easily, but mine grasp of her language would have been woefully inadequate. The very tiny smattering of Hindi I'd picked up from the servants would not have done to discuss Fatalism, laissez faire or any other ism with anybody, let alone a Princess of Badraon or anywhere else, sitting there by the roadside on a mossy stone.

"The fantastic story of my life has just ended today. If you please, I shall tell you it," the Princess said.

11

"Of course," I said, "No question of pleasing. If you want to tell me, my ears will be gratified."

Let nobody think that I spoke these words in Hindi as I have written them down. I wanted to, but my store of the language was sparse, as I've said before. While my Lady was speaking, her words flowed like the morning breeze blowing over a dew-drenched, gold-tipped rice paddy, so humble, so beautiful, so unhindered were the sentences. And I answered her in words so terse, broken-up and piecemeal as to be almost barbarically insolent. The grace and gentility of the language which make it formal were out of my league; I'd never learnt it. For the first time in life, while speaking to my Lady, I felt the meanness of my conduct to the core.

Said she, "On my father's side we were distantly related to the emperor of Delhi. Because we were so high-born, it was difficult to find a suitable bridegroom, who matched our pedigree exactly, for me. Although the Nawab family of Lakhnau had sent a proposal, my father was hesitating; meanwhile the confrontation between the English and the natives over cutting cartridges by the teeth began. The skies over India darkened with smoke from the cannon-fire."

I'd never heard Hindi spoken in a female voice before, let alone from an aristocratic one; hearing it today I understood clearly that this was the diction of the aristocracy—the days when this was commonly spoken had long gone by; today, in this mess of railways, telegraphs, heavy workloads, and the decadence of nobility, everything has shrunk to almost nothing, terse and so direct as to be almost devoid of idioms. Just hearing the Nawabzadi speak awoke in my mind's eye the image of the Mogul emperors' palaces, as if by enchantment—impressive skyscrapers of white stone, horses trotting the roads in ornate saddles and bridles, elephants with gold-fringed howdahs on their backs, citizens with their fantastic headgear of many colors and designs, loose garments of wool, silk or muslin, curved scimitars tucked into their cummerbunds, curved roll-topped gold or silver shoes—long leisure, ample clothing and abundant chivalry.

The Nawabzadi said, "Our fort stood on the left bank of the Yamuna. A Hindu Brahmin named Kesharlal commanded our forces."

The lady poured all the sweet nectar in her voice onto that name Kesharlal, just in that brief moment. Placing my walking-stick on the ground before me, I shifted to make myself more comfortable.

"Kesharlal was a devout Hindu. Rising early every morning, I'd look out my bedroom window at Kesharlal, up to his neck in the night-chilled water, walking clockwise in circles chanting the mantras with folded hands to offer anjali to the dawn. Then he'd sit on the bank in wet clothes and after praying intently in silence for a time, wend homeward singing bhajans in the morning raga of Bhairon, in that superbly melodious voice of his.

I was a Muslim lass, but no one had taught me anything about my religion, and I had no idea how to pray or fast in the Islamic way. In those days, luxurious living, a propensity to drink too much and laissez faire had made the religious foundation of even our men lax and permissive. Nor was a religious atmosphere prevalent in the harem.

Perhaps God Almighty Himself had infused into me a natural thirst for religion, or I don't know if any other reason existed. However, the sight of Kesharlal performing his act of worship on the riverbank on those cool early morns filled my just-awakened heart with a sort of sweet reverence.

Controlled living had infused Kesharlal's fair lively form with a comeliness that made him shine out like a smokeless flame. The greatness of that Brahmin good would fill this Muslim girl's foolish heart with tenderness.

I had a Hindu maid, who would go every day to kiss Kesharlal's feet and so pay her respects; I'd be both glad and envious to see this. On special occasions this serving maid of mine would feed Brahmins and give alms. I'd give her money from my own purse and ask, "Why, my lass, won't you invite Kesharlal?"

At this she'd bite her tongue and say, "Kesharlalthakur doesn't accept alms or handouts from anyone."

So, not being able to show Kesharlal any mark of respect directly or indirectly, my heart would hunger disconsolately.

An ancestor of ours had forced a Brahmin girl to marry him. Sitting at the rim of our inner court, I could feel her pure blood flowing in my own veins, and by dint of that, feel a closeness to Kesharlal and be somewhat satisfied.

From my Hindu serving maid, I learnt as much of Hindu customs, the fantastic tales of their deities, the Ramayana and the Mahabharata from end to end, and imagined the strangely beautiful scenes in my young mind. The idols small and large, the sounds from conchs and bells, the temples with their gold turrets, the acrid yet fragrant smoke from the incense, the aroma from the flowers daubed with sandalwood paste, the supernatural powers of yogis and ascetics, the inhuman goodness of the Brahmins, The strange machinations of deities in human guise, all would mingle and blend together in my mind, fashioning for me a very ancient, very vast, very faraway, extraordinary fairy world; my heart would flit around like a bird in the palace at dusk, without a nest to come home to. The Hindu household was to my girlish heart a very beautiful fairyland.

At this time a conflict erupted between the Company and the sipahis. The waves of it stirred our little fort at Badraon, too.

Said Kesharlal, "Now we shall rout out those beef-eating British folk from Aryavarta and start gambling for the Kingdom between the Hindus and the Muslims."

My father, Ghulam Quadir Khan, was a very cautious person; terming the English by a special form of kinship, he stated, "These people can work miracles. The people of Hindustan can never stand up to them. I won't fight the Company, because I can't lose this mine little fort over an uncertainty."

When the blood of both the Hindus and the Muslims of Hindustan had almost reached the boiling point, we all despised my father for his merchant-like caution. Even my Begum mothers were agitated.

Meanwhile Kesharlal arrived with sizable armed forces and told my father, "My dear Nawab sahib, if you don't join our side, I'll capture you and keep you prisoner as long as this battle goes on, taking over this fort as well."

"You don't have to do anything," said Papa, "I'm on your side, believe you me."

"We have to have some money from the treasury," said Kesharlal.

Papa did not give much. "I'll give as much as I can, when and where needed," said he.

I gathered up all the jewelry I had, from my head to my toes, tied them up securely in a cloth bundle, and secretly sent them on to Kesharlal by my Hindu maid. He accepted it. The pleasurable thrill of this made the hair on my unadorned body stand on end.

Kesharlal set to cleaning up the old rusty swords and rifles; in the meantime, the British Commissioner of the indigo factory rode into our fort in a cloud of dust with a contingent of redcoats. My father, Ghulam Quadir Khan, had secretly informed them of a brewing rebellion.

Kesharlal had a supernatural hold on the forces of Badraon, so much so that each and every soldier there stood ready to make the ultimate sacrifice, even with broken guns and dulled swords, at his word alone.

The home of my treacherous father became for me a living hell. Sorrow and resentment, embarrassment and yes, the gall of hate too, filled my young heart yet not a tear did I shed. Disguising myself in the garb of my timid brother, I left the palace, so quietly that no one noticed.

On the battlefield, the dust, the smoke from the gunpowder, the cries of the soldiers and the rattle of gunfire had given way to the awful stillness of death, pervading land, air and sea. The sun had set, flushing the waters of the Yamuna a bright red. In the unclouded evening sky the nearly-full moon shimmered softly.

The battlefield was full of the horrible scenes of death. At any other time, my heart would have filled with pity, but that night I roamed the battlefield as one in a dream, my eyes seeking Kesharlal all the while. That was my only goal; everything else paled to insignificance beside it.

Searching and then looking again for him, I spied not far from the battlefield the corpses of Kesharlal and his devoted manservant, Deokinandan, by the bright light of the midnight moon. I understood that being grievously wounded, either the master had borne the servant, or the servant the master, to this safe haven, only to succumb to death in peace.

The first thing I did was to satisfy my long-held craving. I opened out my knee-length tresses and wiped the dust from his feet over and over with them. I raised his stone-cold feet to my forehead, and upon kissing them my tears, held at bay so long, spilled right over.

Now Kesharlal's body twitched, and hearing a groan of utter pain, I started from his feet. I heard him say once in a parched voice, his eyes closed, "Water."

Right then I wet my dress in the nearby waters of the Yamuna and virtually ran back. I wrung water out of my saturated dress into Kesharlal's half-closed lips, and tended the grievous injury to his forehead that had taken out his left eye, bandaging it up with a strip torn off my wet attire.

15

After I had splashed water on his face like that a few more times, he stirred and slowly woke up out of his swoon. "Do you need more water?" I asked.

"Who are you?" He asked in return.

"This captive maid of yours is your devoted servant," I replied, "I am the daughter of Nawab Ghulam Quadir Khan." I'd thought that the idea of Kesharlal's taking my final introduction to his grave was a pleasure no one had the power to deprive me of.

As soon as I said that, Kesharlal sat right up, despite his weakness, and slapped me so hard on the cheek that for a moment I almost fainted and saw stars, "Daughter of the infidel! Irreligious one! Thou defile my religion by offering me water from thy Muslim hands?"

I was then but sixteen, and it was my first day out of the harem; the greedy sun burning in the sky overhead hadn't managed to steal the roses from my lovely cheeks. On first coming out, this was the first greeting I got from the world and from mine deity.

My cigarette had gone out, and I sat entranced, as still as a picture. I know not whether I was listening to a story, a poem or just the spoken word. I sat speechless. At long last, unable to contain myself, I cried out, "The beast!"

"What beast?" Was the Princess' quick repartee, "Does even a beast refuse water when he's parching with thirst?"

"That's so," I was a bit nonplussed, "Then he's a deity."

"Deity?" quipped the Princess with a derisive smile, "What deity would refuse his devotee's sincere worship?"

"You know, that's right!" I concurred, and fell silent.

The Princess went on with her tale, "At first my feelings were grievously hurt. It seemed as if the world had fallen into pieces over my head. Regaining my senses in a moment, I bowed at the feet of that cruel, hard-hearted, stony, pure, stoic Brahmin from afar—I said to myself, 'O Brahmin, thou accept neither the ministrations of the lowly, the food of others, donations from the wealthy, nor the youth of a young lady. Thou art so different by thine lone self, so aloof and distant, I haven't even the right to surrender to thee.'"

I cannot really tell what Kesharlal thought about the Princess bowing to the ground to kiss his feet like that. His face was a mask of stoicism. Looking quietly at my face just once, he then rose slowly to his full height. I was alert to put out my hand to support him. He refused silently and with painful halting steps walked to the bank of the Yamuna. There was a little ferryboat tied up to the dock. There was neither boatman nor passenger in it. Getting into this very teeny boat, Kesharlal weighed anchor. In the wink of an eye, the boat sailed mid-river and then slowly out of sight—I wished to fold my hands to that invisible mini-boat with all my heartache, all my youth, all my spurned respect that quiet moonlit night and drown myself in the still waters of the Yamuna like a full-blown flower shorn untimely from her stem, and so give up this useless life."

"However, this I could not do. That full moon, the dark copses on the banks of the Yamuna, the still, dark-blue waters of the Kalindi, far off over the mango grove the spire of our fort sparkling in the moonlight, all sang to me of death in silent concert. That night the three worlds shimmering in the moonlight all enticed me to death. Only that tiny shell of a boat, so dilapidated it could hardly stay afloat, called me back and tore me away from that peaceful, beautiful, dignified, endless, world-pleasing death to the path of life. Like one in a trance I walked the banks of the Yamuna through cattail swamps, deserts, stony banks and woods dense with shrubbery.

Here the speaker fell silent. I too did not speak.

After a very long while the Princess caught up the thread of her story, "After this the story begins to get complicated. How I can analyze it or tell it lucidly, I have absolutely no idea. I had begun my quest through a dense tangled forest, exactly which path I'd chosen to follow I could not now seek out. Where should I begin or end, what should I reject and what should I take along, how can I make it perfectly clear so that naught seems improbable?

However, these last few days of my life have taught me that nothing is impossible. To a Princess fresh from the harem, the outside world may seem difficult to navigate, but that is entirely a figment of the imagination. Once she comes out, the path presents itself; it may not be the Nawabi one, but it is a path nonetheless. People have trod that path through the ages—it is endless, hard and sometimes queer indeed, branching off in many directions; joys and sorrows, hindrances and blockages make it sometimes dangerous, but there it is—a path.

A lone Princess' journey along this path of common usage hardly makes a good story, and even if it did, I would not be interested in telling it. In one word, I've suffered so much, yet life did not become intolerable. Like a firecracker I burnt brighter as I flew higher. As I sped along I did not feel myself burning out. Now suddenly the fire that stoked my joy and sorrow has gone black out, and here I am, like an inanimate object fallen onto the dust by the wayside—today my journey is over, and here ends my tale, too."

So saying, the Princess ceased. Secretly I shook my head; it cannot end here like this. Keeping quiet a bit I requested in Hindi very broken up indeed, "Pardon me, Your Highness. Excuse my asking, but could you elaborate a bit on the ending? It'd mitigate mine agitation."

The Princess smiled. I saw that my broken up Hindi had borne fruit. If I'd talked in aristocratic diction she'd have been much more reticent, but just the knowledge that I know only a smattering of her mother-tongue lent a distance and acted as the curtain between us.

I could not take all this anymore. Leaving my Guru's abode, I dressed as a Bhairavi and ventured out. I've roamed all over everywhere, on roads, shrines, mission houses and temples. I couldn't find Kesharlal anywhere. The few who knew him by name would say, "He's dead, either by royal decree or in battle." My heart told me, "Certainly not. Kesharlal cannot die. That Brahmin, that intolerably searing fire hasn't been put out yet. He's still out there, burning bright, to receive mine offering, at some remote yagna altar."

In the Hindu Scriptures, there are mentioned Sudras who became Brahmins by austere meditation; whether Muslims can turn Brahmin it never says, the only reason being simply that there were no Muslims at the time. I knew that my meeting with Kesharlal was still very far off, because before that I had to turn Brahmin. One by one, thirty years went by. I became a Brahmin through and through. The blood of my long-ago Brahmin grandmother coursed through my veins full force. I established myself at the feet of that first Brahmin of the start of my youth, that very last Brahmin of the end of my youth, the only Brahmin of my three worlds, and gained an unforeseen glow.

I'd heard much of Kesharlal's bravery in battle, but that did not imprint itself on my heart. The image I'd seen of poor Kesharlal quietly floating away by his lone self on the silent full-moon night in that pea-shell of a boat, is etched clearly in my mind. I kept seeing the Brahmin floating on the lonely current night and day towards some mystery—he has no companions, no manservant, he needs no one, that purely self-contained man is fulfilled with himself. The stars in the Heavens observe him silently.

In the meantime I got the news that Kesharlal had eluded the King's punishment and taken refuge in Nepal. I too hied myself there. After living there for a long time, I heard that Kesharlal had left Nepal long ago, and where he was right then nobody knew.

Then I began traveling these hills. This is no Hindu country. These Bhutiyas and Lepchas are infidels, they do not care what they eat, their deities and methods of worship are very different from those of other religions; I was afraid lest the purity I'd obtained after such hard labor be sullied in any way. I tried very hard to keep away from anything impure. I knew my port was near, my life's ultimate shrine wasn't so far off anymore.

And then, what can I say after that? The conclusion is so very brief. When the lamp is dim, one breath can extinguish it, what takes a long explanation?

After thirty-eight long years, I'm here in Darjeeling and I found Kesharlal this morning."

Hearing the speaker stop here I asked eagerly, "Yes? What did you see?"

"I saw," said the Princess, "Old Kesharlal, in dirty clothes and with downcast face, in the Bhutiya village shucking corn with his wife and children."

The story ended. I thought a consoling word or two were in order. Said I, "He who's had to live in fear for his life continually for thirty-eight long years cannot keep his rituals intact, now can he?"

"You think I don't get that?" the Princess said, "But what was I running after, all these years? How was I to know that the actions of the Brahmin who had stolen my adolescent heart were meaningless rituals, done by rote? To me that was religion, without beginning or end. If it were not so, how could I surrender my young, beautiful self at sixteen, so innocent and flower-like, so softly, sweetly devoted, to that Brahmin, have been so soundly berated and borne it all so quietly as my due over my head in twice the respect? O Brahmin, thou hast found another habit in lieu of the one thou lost, yet where can I find another life, another youth for the life and youth that are no longer mine?"

So saying, the lady stood up, "Namashkar Babuji!"

19

Then just in the next instant she seemed to correct herself, "Salam Babu Sahib!" By this Muslim goodbye, she seemed to bid farewell to the rickety, broken Brahmin lying in the dust. Before I could speak she seemed to blend like a cloud into the thick gray fog of the summit.

Closing my eyes for a moment, I began to see the whole scene in my mind's eye like a picture. The image of the beautiful little Princess sitting luxuriously on a velvet cushion at her bedroom window in the fort, of the older woman on pilgrimage so saturated with devotion at Vespers, and then here in this mountain retreat of Darjeeling, beside Calcutta Road, the old brokenhearted woman devoid of all hope, enveloped in the fog—The conflict of the opposing flows of Brahmin and Muslim blood in that comely woman's form gave rise to a strangely haunting melody in beautiful complete Urdu, melting and pulsing in my brain.

Opening my eyes, I saw that the misty clouds had given way to pleasant sunshine bathing the clear sky. The British ladies in their push-carts and the gentlemen on horseback had come out to take the air, among them a very few Bengalis muffled in their scarves, who were smilingly looking askance at me.

I got up out of there very quickly indeed. In this brightly sunlit landscape, that cloudy tale did not ring true at all. I believe I'd mixed the smoke from my cigarette copiously into the mountain mist and just made up this piece—that Muslim-Brahmin lady, that hero, and that fort on the bank of the Yamuna, nothing may have been real.

3   DIRE NEGLECT (ORIGINAL: HAIMANTI)

This is the story of a child-marriage, and of a bride who, because she happened to be older than the norm during those times, was neglected and humiliated.

THE BRIDE'S FATHER could have waited, but the bridegroom's father had no wish to, for he could see that the girl was fast passing the age of marriage, and a few more years would make that very much a thorn on the side. It is true that this bride-to-be was older than most, but the specific gravity of her dowry rose proportionately—and thus the haste.

Who, you may ask, was the bridegroom? I confess unabashedly that it was I; so, my elders deemed it unnecessary to seek my input on the subject. I had done my work—passed my F. A. examinations and received a scholarship to continue my college education. As such, Hymen's two parties—the bride's party and the bridegroom's party—were in a perfect flutter of agitation over me.

In this land of ours, a man once married has no anxiety over it. He regards his wife just as a tiger that has once tasted of human flesh and blood would, with nonchalant incuriosity about its texture and taste. Whatever his situation or age, once he loses a wife through death or divorce, he has no hesitation filling her place with another. All prerogatives of hesitation, embarrassment and anxiety seem to belong to us, the younger generation. Repeated marriage-proposals turn their fathers' hair back with hair-dye to black from ash-gray, and these youth go gray in one night with anxiety at the hint of a marriage.

To tell the truth, such anxieties plagued me not in the least. On the contrary, this marriage proposal blew right into my heart like the southern breeze, where its curious whisperings hummed eagerly. For someone who has to memorize five to seven volumes of notes on Burke's French Revolution, this attitude is reprehensible. I would have to be more cautious if my article were to be approved by the Textbook Board.

But oh, what am I doing? Is this a story or a novel that I have set out to write? I had no idea when I began to write that my article would assume this tone. I had only wanted to dispel the fog of pain that had shrouded my mind for the last few years by the torrents of a nor'easter shower; however, neither could I write Bengali children's books, for I hadn't the grammatical prowess needed for such a project, nor indeed could I venture into poetry, because I seem to myself not to have enough imagination to let my thoughts bloom into poetical expressions. As such I see the hermit inside me bursting into peals and peals of unrestrained laughter. What else could he do? The well of his tears has run dry; any attempt at weeping would make his eyes crack and burn, just like the earth in the searing, blistering heat of a drought-stricken summer.

I won't reveal the real name of my wife, because it is no subject for archaeologists to mull over. The only copperplate on which it is indelibly etched is my bleeding heart. I can hardly bring myself to imagine the day when that name and that plate would sink into oblivion forever. However, perhaps no historian has ever been to the Eden where it is eternal, never to be rubbed off or forgotten.

But for this story she needs a name, whatever it may be. All right then, let me call her Shishir (Dew), because in a dewdrop combine the tears of the night coolness and the smile of the morning sunlight, drying up completely as the sun gets hotter.

Shishir was two years younger than I, but it was not for that reason that my own father did not like child-marriages. His father, it was said, had been a total nonconformist, so much so as to have been considered an outcast. He had been thoroughly English-educated. My father, on the other hand, is a rigid conformist. It's almost impossible to find anything in or around our home and the neighborhood that he does not try his utmost to conform to, for he too had studied English extensively. Both he and my grandfather held opinions that protested against social norms and conventions; none was simply natural. Even so, the reason for my father's consenting to my tying the knot with a considerably older girl was that the older the bride, the more the dowry. Shishir was an only child, so my father believed that the high dowry would be filling my future coffers.

My father-in-law held no fixed opinions. He had a stable job under a tribal chief in the Western Hills. Shishir's mother had died when Shishir was just about a year old. She was getting older year by year, but her father turned a blind eye to this. There was no one around to point this out specifically to him.

In due time Shishir turned sixteen by nature, not by social standards. No one had cautioned her about her age, so she was not overly conscious of it.

At nineteen, I had just been promoted to my junior year at college, when the rose of marriage bloomed for me. Whether nineteen is a suitable age for marriage may be a topic for debate among social reformers, but if you ask me, that age is as appropriate for marriage as for passing examinations.

The wedding sun rose at the hint of a photograph. While I was hard at study, a very close relative placed that photo right in my line of sight and remarked laughingly, "Now comes some real studying, so jump into it, my dear lad!"

A novice photographer had taken the picture. As Shishir had no mother, no one had made her up with lots of cosmetics, fancy clothes or an elaborate hairdo wrapped in gold or silver ribbon. The face that looked back at me was pretty in a quiet sort of way, with clear eyes that held the mirth of a young life in check. She wore a simple sari, but in that very simplicity was a dignity I cannot for the world describe adequately. She sat on a rickety stool with a striped poncho behind her; there was a small vase of flowers on a side-table beside her, and resting on the carpet under the curved border of her sari were two bare brown feet.

The moment my eyes fell on that picture, it felt as if Cupid had shot me through with one of his fatal arrows, or as if some magician had waved his golden wand of love over me. Those clear eyes seemed to look beyond the physical me and right into my innermost thoughts;

those two bare brown feet under that curved border walked right into my heart and planted themselves firmly there.

Days passed by; two or three opportune moments came and went, but my future father-in-law could not obtain leave of absence. In the meantime unlucky moments threatened to push me unnecessarily to my twentieth year. The thought made me burn with resentment towards my future father-in-law and towards his boss.

Anyway, my wedding-day fell on the very end of the opportune period. How clearly I remember every note the oboe played that evening! All my waking hours have been touched by every moment of that beautiful night. Long live the age of nineteen!

Amidst all the noise and merry-making of the wedding-party, the bride's father gave her away, and her soft cool hand was laid over mine. Could there ever be anything else as wonderful as that? "I've got her; I really have," I repeated to myself over and over.

But whom indeed had I got? She was rare, human and unceasingly mysterious. My father-in-law, named Gaurisankar, seemed to be the namesake of the Himalayas on whose lap he spent his days. At the very crest of his serenity glowed a pure, radiant smile showing he was at peace with the world, and from his heart gushed such a fountain of love that those who came in contact with him never wanted to let him go.

Before returning to his workplace, Papa took me aside and whispered, "My son, I've brought up my little girl for seventeen years. You I've known only this very short while, yet I leave my sweet one in your hands. Learn to appreciate the gem she is; there is no way for me to bless you any more than that."

Everyone, my parents included, told him, "Please don't worry; in leaving her father, your daughter has gained a family here."

Papa smiled sadly on taking his daughter's leave and said, "Sweetheart, I have to go now. This is your only father, and if from now on he loses, spoils or has purloined anything at all, it won't be my fault."

Said the daughter, "Oh yes? But make sure you cut those losses."

At last, just before he left, she cautioned him about his habitual lapses of food habits. Papa was not cautious enough of what he ate; some forbidden and restricted foods were among his especial favorites. Shishir's special duty had been to steer her father clear of those foods.

So now, holding onto his right hand, she anxiously implored, "Papa, please won't you listen to me?"

Smiling sadly, the father replied, "Promises are made only to be broken. So, to be safe, I won't promise."

After saying goodbye to her father, Shishir locked herself into our bedroom; what happened in there is anyone's guess.

At this seemingly tearless parting our women, including Ma, my aunts and others, who had seen and heard it from an adjoining room, were flabbergasted. How really astonishing! The dry climate out west had dried up her affections!

Mr. Banamali, a very close friend of my father-in-law's, had been the go-between in our marriage. Everyone in our family knew him well also. He'd told his friend, "You have just this one little daughter in the world. So, come live here and spend the rest of your life near her."

Said Papa, "What I've given I've given away entirely. If I look back now I shall be hurt. There is no embarrassment greater than that of being where I'm not wanted."

To end it all, Papa took me aside and whispered shyly like a big plotter, "My baby likes to entertain people from time to time, and she also likes to read good books. Would your father mind if I send some money for her now and then?"

I was rather taken aback at this question. Truth be told, I'd never seen my parents callous enough to look down on extra money, wherever it came from and whenever it came.

Putting a hundred-rupee bill in the palm of my right hand as secretly as if he were bribing me, Papa left hurriedly before I could thank him or say goodbye. Looking on from behind, now at last I saw him take out his handkerchief.

Sitting stock-still, I could not help thinking that these simple yet lofty mountain-dwellers were cast in a mold totally different from us plains folk.

I have seen many friends tie the knot. Right after the ceremony, the bride seems to be swallowed whole. A while after being digested, she re-emerges in her true colors. There may be some hint of internal discomfort, but the road down is as sharply clear and slippery as crystal. I had realized right while I was taking my vows that the wife I got by doing this might be enough for household chores, but most of her remains unknown. I feel that most people just get married and go through life without earning their wives' love, not even realizing what they missed out on. The wives never find out either. But she was my jewel among women, rare and precious, glowing with inner beauty and strength—not chattel or property at all, but a dear and valued companion on life's journey onward.

Shishir—no, I won't use that name any more, for firstly that wasn't her real name at all, and secondly it doesn't even begin to describe her. She is as constant as the sun, not as transient as the tears of rosy Aurora. Why conceal anymore the fact that her real name was Haimanti?

I observed that although this seventeen-year-old had the sun of adulthood shining on her, she was in some respects still an adolescent, yea, even a child, just as the sun when it first rises sends forth rays that yet fail to melt the polar ice cap. I know how intensely pure and untainted my virgin bride was.

Because Haimanti was an older bride, high school educated, I was somewhat anxious about ways of pleasing her. However, in a very short while my anxiety was allayed; to please her was simply to share gladly some of the things she enjoyed. The way into her heart was through the corner bookstore, where I could purchase inexpensive books for her. I don't seem to recall when the first rosy hues of love began to color her heart and mind, dreams of a future rosier than an unclouded dawn shone forth from her tranquil eyes and her whole being became alert; that, however, is only one side of the story. The other side, hitherto untold, can now be elaborated on.

Papa was in the employ of a tribal chief of some importance. The rumors about his bank balance circulated widely. They varied from person to person, but none placed it below one lakh rupees. As a result, the more her father's monetary value increased, the dearer Haimanti became to my family. She was eager to learn our ways, but Mother never let her. Even the maid who had been sent with her, though barred from the bedroom, was never criticized, lest she answer back.

The days could have gone by like this, but one afternoon Father's face suddenly clouded over. It was just this: at Haimanti's and my wedding, Papa had given five thousand rupees' worth of jewelry and fifteen thousand cash. Father had learnt recently from a broker friend of his that the cash had all been borrowed, and at exorbitant rates of interest. The rumor of lakhs of rupees was indeed baseless.

Though the question of money had never been raised with Papa, I know not how my father decided that Papa had intentionally defrauded him.

Then, my father had a preconceived notion that Papa was the Prime Minister of the state, or something like that. On enquiry he found out that Papa was "Only" the head of the Department of Education. Said Father, "Which means a schoolmaster—that most lowly of prestigious jobs." Father had had hopes of my succeeding Papa after his retirement.

In the meantime the chariot-fair that signals autumn rolled around, and relatives from our village homestead began to converge on our Calcutta home. Once they laid eyes on Haimanti, they began to whisper, louder and louder every time. A distant great-aunt called, "Oh, dear Lord! The bride is even older than I am!"

Another great-aunt remarked, "If Apu had wanted a younger bride, he could have found one right here!"

My mother said loudly, "Oh, what a thing to say! She is but eleven, going on twelve. She grew up so robust on bread and soup out west."

"Dearie, I still see well enough. The bride's father must have concealed her age."

"But we saw the horoscope," my mother persisted. This was very true, but the horoscope itself was proof that Haimanti was seventeen, and not twelve as everyone else averred.

"But can't a horoscope lie, even?" the old ladies were not to be deterred. This brought on a bitter argument, and even precipitated a quarrel that threatened to tear the family apart.

In the meantime, in came none other than Haimanti herself. Some grandma asked, "How old are you, Sweetie?"

Mama winked a signal; uncomprehending, Haima answered truthfully, "Seventeen."Agitated, Ma countered, "You don't know."

"I know I'm seventeen, as surely as I know I'm standing here," insisted Haimanti.

The Grandmas fell silent, nudging each other; flabbergasted and angry at her daughter-in-law's naiveté, my mother retorted, "As if you know all! Your father told us himself, and you say 'certainly not!'"

This was news to Haima. Startled, she said unbelievingly, "Papa said that? But . . . but he couldn't have!"

"What a surprise! Her father said it himself in front of all of us, and she has the gall to deny it!" asserted Mama, and winked again.

Now at last, comprehension dawned on Haima. Strengthening her voice, she declaimed, "Papa could never declare a thing like that publicly."

"Oh, so you're calling me a liar?" screamed Mother, her voice rising to a crescendo.

"My father would never lie," Haima was undeterred.

The more Mother screamed and scolded after that, the greater the embarrassment became.

Mother complained to Father about Haima's foolish stubbornness. Calling her to him, Father reprimanded, "You don't need to declare to the world that at seventeen you're still unmarried. This is nothing to be proud of . . . . I tell you, this can't go on here."

Oh, how had my father's affectionate tone to Haima roughened up so?

Saddened, Haima asked, "If anyone asks about my age, how do I answer?"

"Tell them your mother-in-law knows," said Father. Hearing his explanation of how not to lie, Haima fell silent in such a way that my father knew his advice had gone totally west.

Instead of feeling sorry for Haima, I was too embarrassed to look her in the eye. That day I saw her eyes, clear and distant as the autumn morn, take on a hunted look; like a doe fleeing a hunter's gun, she looked up at me and thought, "I don't recognize these people."

Just that afternoon, I had bought her a Morocco-bound, gold-embossed edition of Tennyson's poems. She took it and slowly put it on her lap without opening it.

Taking her hand, I declared, "Haima my love, please don't be angry at me. I am bound to you in truth; by that truth I swear never to hurt you."

Haima smiled the slow silent smile of one who knows. For those blessed with such a smile, there need be no words.

Since the financial upswing, interest in religion and its observances had revived in our home. Until now, Haima had had no part in these. But one evening she was told to prepare the altar; she said, "Ma, show me how, please!"

This was no surprise, because everyone was well aware that the motherless Haima had been brought up outside Bengal. The object of this command, however, was to embarrass her. Everyone remarked, "Oh, my God, what is this? She must be from a godless house. The prosperity of this home cannot be long now, for sure."

At this, Papa was called some unmentionable names. Until now, whenever anything bad or embarrassing had come up, Haima had borne it silently; she hadn't even cried openly. But today her feelings were so badly hurt that she burst into tears and choked out, "You know that everyone in that region calls Papa a saint?"

A saint, indeed! This comment did nothing but provoke uproarious laughter of derision.

From then on everyone referred to Papa as "that saintly father of yours". They had found the tender spot in this young woman's heart.

In reality, Papa was neither a Brahma nor a Christian; he held no fixed religious beliefs or convictions. He simply had never thought about strict religious observances. He had taught his daughter many things but that. "I can't teach her what I don't know," he had answered a friend's question, "That would be cheating."

The only person who befriended Haima in our house was my younger sister, sixteen-year-old Narani. Because she liked her Boudi, she had to endure anger, looks askance and reprimands from everyone else, except me. My sweet little sister would tell me everything that went on in the house; from her I learnt of the slings and arrows of humiliation that Haima endured. But never once did Haima herself complain. She was embarrassed about it, and not for herself either.

All letters from Papa would be shared between us; they were short but sweet, tender and interesting. She would have me read her replies to him, too. Our conjugal life seemed incomplete without this. There was no hint of a complaint about our house in any letter of hers; if there had been, problems too knotty to fix might have arisen. As it were, we were drowning in a sea of trouble already. I had heard from Narani that some of Haima's letters were opened to find out what she had written about us.

Finding nothing to scold about in her letters, my family, instead of cooling down, adopted a different tactic; perhaps they suffered from broken hopes. Very irritated, they began to complain, "Why these frequent letters? As if we didn't matter at all to her." Much mudslinging went on about this. Rather wounded, I suggested to Haima, "From now on, give me all letters you write to Papa. I myself shall mail them on my way to college."

In amazement, Haima asked, "But why?" However, I was too embarrassed to answer.

Everyone at home now started saying, "The girl has taken Apu's mind over. The degree is out of reach, and through no fault of his, either."

It seemed that Haima was blamed for every little thing that went wrong—that she happened to be seventeen and not twelve, that I loved her and that by God's decree her love sang in my heart.

I could very well have flung my degree remorselessly west. However, for Haima's sake I vowed to graduate—and with honors to boot. In that agitated state of mind I could have kept my vow for two reasons, one that the books I needed to study for my courses could very well have been shared with Haima, and the other, that Haima's love was too great to bind me.

I began to prepare for my exams in dead earnest; one Sunday around noon I was at my desk, engrossed in Martineau's Theory of Characters. Looking up momentarily, I saw Haima sitting at one of the windows that were set into the rails of the curved wooden staircase at the northern end of our courtyard, which led to the upper rooms. There sat Haima, looking out onto our neighbor's yard, where a tree full of fiery pinks contrasted with the verdant green.

Something lifted away the misty veil of misunderstanding from my heart with a wrenching jolt. All this time, the quiet depth of so profound and silent a grief had eluded me.

I could see nothing but her way of sitting there, with both hands folded on her lap, her faraway gaze poignant with longing. She leant against the railing, her open curls falling over her left shoulder and clustering on her breast. My heart cried out.

My own life was filled so to the brim with affection and friendships that I had failed to notice any emptiness in others. Suddenly today a gaping abyss of nothingness opened up right in front of me, threatening to swallow me and everything & everyone I valued. With what could I endeavor to fill that chasm?

I hadn't had to leave anything—family, relatives, friends, old habits and pastimes, anything at all. Haima, on the other hand, had left everything behind to come and be my wife—her beloved father, the mountain home where she had grown up and her former carefree life. I couldn't even begin to fathom how much that was. In our family she had to endure the thorns of humiliation and callous neglect; in a way she and I shared what she went through, not separated. However, this Oread had enjoyed a sublime physical and spiritual liberty for seventeen years. As a result, her nature had become open and simple, gaining from the pure truth and liberal light of the mountains. I hadn't really given a thought to how it must have hurt her to wrench away from all that, because there she and I separated.

Haima was slowly dying from the inside out, every moment. I could give her anything but liberty, something I myself had never had. For this reason she has mute communion with the silent sky from behind the bars of her window; some nights I would wake up to find she had gone from the bed and climbed onto the roof, where she lay with her head on her hands, gazing up at the star-studded sky.

I left Martineau alone and thought hard about a course of action; there was only one thing to do, and I would do it. From a very early age I was shy and a little apprehensive of asking any big favor from Father, so much so as never to face him with a plea. But that day I felt I had to say, "Haima hasn't been feeling herself lately. She should go visit her father for a while" flat out.

My father was dumfounded and very angry, never doubting at all that Haima had put me up to this. Marching indoors right then, he demanded of Haimanti, "I say, what is the matter with you?"

"Nothing," replied Haimanti evasively. Father thought this answer signified arrogance.

But none of us had eyes enough to notice that Haima was wasting away daily. One afternoon, Mr. Banamali came to visit us and remarked, "Oh, Haimi dear, how wan you seem! Are you all right?"

"Ah yes," smiled Haima, "I'm fine."

About ten days after this, Papa himself hied on over suddenly. His friend must have written to him, expressing concern for Haima's health.

After the wedding, Haima had suppressed her tears. But this time, when her father lovingly raised her chin she could keep them back no longer. Papa could not say anything at all, even to ask how things went. He'd noticed something on his little girl's face that was breaking his heart.

Haima led Papa by the hand to the little bedroom she and I shared. She had so many things to ask, especially as Papa himself looked none too well.

"Come with me, my little sweetheart?" Papa asked tenderly.

"Oh, yes, please!" Haima was as eager for freedom as a caged bird.

"All right then; I'll see if I can arrange it," Papa promised sanguinely, but had he not been so anxious about Haima he'd have noticed that things had changed; he had no longer the prestige here that he'd once enjoyed. Father, thinking him an annoyance, behaved in a way that bordered on rudeness. Papa remembered my father's telling him once cordially that he could take Haima home any time he wanted to. He, poor man, had no idea that financial situations played so major a part in a man's prestige, and that words uttered on honor could turn right around so easily.

Puffing away on the hookah, father said, "I have no say in this. If you'd go in . . . ."

I knew full well what "going in" meant; it would be of absolutely no avail. Just as I had supposed, nothing came of this.

Haima, and not well! How unjust an accusation!

Papa himself had a good doctor in to check his daughter up thoroughly. Said the doctor, "This young woman needs a change of scenery, adequate diet and nurturing. Otherwise she may fall deathly ill."

Laughing, my father countered, "Anyone may fall seriously ill. What of that?"

"You know, this doctor is quite reputed," protested Papa, "You shouldn't make light of him."

"I've seen many a doctor in my time, too prepared to diagnose anything for some ready cash," replied my father.

This heartless, callous reply cut Papa to the quick. Haima, standing near, understood that Papa's proposal had been rejected ignominiously. She seemed turned to stone.

Unable to stand any more, I said, "I shall take Haima on a change myself." But my father roared, "Oh no you won't!" etc.

Friends and acquaintances have asked me why I did not do what I said I would. I could very well have taken my wife away by force and left. Why did I not? Well, it was because I could not place truth before custom as was meet, I could not sacrifice my wife to my family. Do you know that I was a part of the crowd that demanded that Sita be sacrificed? I am among those who glorify this ignominy; moreover, I had extolled the virtues of separation in an article recently published in the monthly magazine to please my readers. Who knew then that I would have to endure second separation from my very own Sita, one that would virtually drain my life-blood?

Another moment of parting between father and daughter came. Laughingly the daughter remarked, "Papa dear, if you keep on running back here to see me, I shall have to padlock myself in the bedroom."

Laughing too, Papa replied, "In that case I see I have to bring pick and shovel if I do come again."

After this I never saw on Haima's face that sweet serene smile of hers. What happened even later still, I can hardly write of. I hear my parents are looking for a second wife for me. It is very probable that I may one day give in to my mother's continuous pleas, because . . . . oh, that is another story altogether.

4 SECOND SIGHT
(ORIGINAL: DRISHTIDAAN)

In this story we meet a blind wife whose husband mistreats her, albeit not meaning to. Their marriage comes to the brink of dissolution because he does not consider her feelings when he does something. This is mistreatment, and no wife deserves to be treated so.

THE SAYING GOES that many marriageable women nowadays have to seek out mates for themselves. I too have done this, but the deities were on my side; I had worshipped Shiva many times since I was a small girl, and performed numerous rituals.

I was not yet eight when I was married; however, perhaps owing to sins from a past life, I could not get this husband of mine wholly to myself. Mother Trinayani took my eyes, leaving my ardent desire to see my husband unfulfilled.

My trials and tribulations began soon after I was married. Before I turned fourteen, I had a stillborn baby; I was near death myself. However, those who have to suffer don't die so easily, just as a lamp full of oil may take an entire night to burn out.

I lived, but physical weakness, and maybe mental strain too, affected my eyes.

My husband was then studying to be an opthalmologist; he would be very happy to try his newly acquired knowledge on anyone at all. So it was he who became my physician.

My elder brother was after a B.L. degree from the local college that year. One day he came to see us, and reprimanded my husband, "What are you doing? If you go on like this, Kumu will lose her eyesight. Get a renowned ophthalmologist to examine her."

"What better treatment would a renowned ophthalmologist recommend? I know the medicine she needs," my husband said.

Somewhat angry, Dada countered, "Then you are no different from your boss at the office."

"What would you, a law student, know about medicine?" my husband shot right back, "If, after you marry, there is a court case over your wife's property, would you come to me for advice?"

I sat there thinking to myself, when there is a big upset, the little people are the ones who suffer. There my husband and brother were at odds, and on both accounts it was I who suffered. Then again I surmised, if my father's family has given me away, why do they want to butt in where their input is not welcome? My husband alone will have to bear the brunt of what happens to me now.

That afternoon, this petty topic of the treatment for my eyes caused a minor rift between Dada and my husband. My eyes would water easily nowadays, so when the watering seemed to get worse, no one, least of all Dada or my husband, could guess the reason.

A little later, when my husband had left for college, Dada returned with an ophthalmologist. He examined my eyes and cautioned me to be extra careful, or they would deteriorate; then he wrote out a prescription, which Dada sent out for right away.

When the doctor had left, I told Dada, "Please, Dada, I beg you, don't interfere with the treatment for my eyes."

From early childhood I had been very afraid of Dada, so that the fact that I could muster the courage to confront him like this was in itself extraordinary; however, I realized that the treatment Dada had initiated for me, unbeknownst to my husband, could only cause harm.

Dada too was perhaps taken a bit aback at my forwardness. Pondering silently for a while, he at last spoke, saying slowly, "Well, okay. I won't bring over any more doctors; but dearie, please use the medicine he prescribed as directed."

When the medicine was brought, Dada explained to me how it was to be used and then left. Before my husband came home from college, I dropped the entire package, prescription, medicine and all, into the well in our courtyard.

Being a bit upset at Dada, my husband redoubled his efforts at treating my eyes. Prescriptions changed morning and evening. I wore monocles and glasses, used eye-drops and powders, and even when foul-smelling cod liver oil nauseated me I hid that from the world. My husband would often ask me how I felt. I'd reply that I was getting much better. I tried hard to convince myself it was so, too. When my eyes would water profusely I thought that these tears would wash out the disease; when the tears stopped I thought it wouldn't be long until my eyes would be cured.

However, in a short while, the pain became unbearable. I began to see everything as if through a haze and to suffer the most excruciating headaches imaginable. I saw that my husband too was nonplussed; he could find no suitable excuse to call another doctor in at this late stage.

I said to him, "Why not call a doctor in, just to please Dada? He is griping needlessly over this, and that really bothers me; you are the one who will treat me, but a second opinion is always a good idea."

"You, as always, are so right, dear heart," agreed my husband, and right that afternoon fetched an English ophthalmologist. I don't know what they discussed, but I think the doctor reprimanded my husband quite a bit; he stood silently by with his head bowed.

When the doctor had left, I took my husband's right hand in both mine and said, "What did you have to go get a British doctor for? He won't understand my eye-trouble any more than you do. You could very easily have called in an Indian doctor, you know."

Rather nonplussed, my husband confessed, "You need eye surgery, my love!"

Feigning a little anger, I shot back, "You knew all along that I'd need eye surgery sooner or later, but you hid it from me. Did you think I'd be scared?"

"Is there a man big enough not to be scared stiff of eye surgery?" my husband said, casting his embarrassment away.

"A man is brave only to his wife," I could not help teasing.

My husband, becoming very serious indeed, concurred, "That's right, of course. A man has only his vanity to uphold."

Flinging solemnity to the winds in assumed nonchalance, I replied, "You are no equals to women in vanity, either. So you see, we win there too."

When Dada came to see us the next time, I called him apart and said, "Dada, the medicine the doctor you brought prescribed was helping quite a bit. But one day by mistake I put my oral medicine into my eyes and now they're real bad. My husband says I need eye surgery."

"I thought thy husband was treating thee all this while," said Dada contritely, "I was hurt and didn't come."

"No," I answered, "I was secretly following that prescription without telling my husband, lest he get angry."

What a tangled web of falsehood and deceit we women do have to weave! I could no sooner hurt Dada than upset my husband. As mothers, we have to cajole our children; as wives, we have to shield our husbands—we have to resort to so many ruses!

As a result of this subterfuge, I saw Dada and my husband restored to friendship before my physical world went totally dark. Dada thought that trying to treat me in secret led to this mishap; my husband repented not having listened to him earlier. So these two repentant souls sought each other's pardon by edging closer and seeking each other's advice when needed.

Then, one morning, according to their compromise, a British eye-surgeon operated on my left eye. That weak organ could not take the strain, and the little sight it had was extinguished suddenly. Little by little, the other eye too lost its sight. A permanent shroud fell upon the sandalwood-decorated, handsome, happy young face that I'd laid eyes on, on my wedding night all those years ago.

One day, my husband came to my bedside and said, "I won't beat about the bush, honey; I'm the one who made you go blind."

I heard his usually crisp voice, so wet with tears it sounded soggy. Taking his right hand in both mine, I said, "That's all right; you've only taken back what was really yours all along. Think about it, if another doctor had made this happen, how would I have consoled myself? Destiny has willed it so, and no one could have saved my eyes. The only solace in my blindness is that mine eyes went in your hands. When he hadn't enough lotuses to offer to the goddess, Ramachandra gouged his eyes out to make up the difference. I dedicate mine sight to mine own deity—my moonlit nights, my first lights of dawns, the blue of my sky, the green of the earth around me, all these I give to you. When you see something that pleases you, describe it to me, and I shall think I've seen it too."

I couldn't say all this as it's depicted here; one can hardly ever speak so coherently. I'd thought these things out long and hard. When exhaustion hit from time to time, my resolve would try to fall apart, I would feel neglected, sad and ill treated by Lady Luck, and I would repeat these words to myself. Relying upon this peace, this reverence, I would try to rise above my trials and tribulations. That day I had probably succeeded a little by words and gestures to show him how I felt. Said he, "Kumu dear, I cannot give back what I've destroyed; but I'll stay right by you, and help you as far as I can."

"That won't do at all," I replied, "I won't let you turn our home into a hospital for the blind. You must marry again." I almost choked before I could elaborate on the reason for his remarriage. After clearing my throat and coughing a few times, I was about to speak when my husband spoke, his voice thick with emotion, "I am a silly fool, and vain to boot. But I am no beast. I blinded you with my own hands; now if I leave you for another wife on top of everything, pray God I may be accused of patricide and Brahmicide."

I wouldn't have let him swear so big an oath; I'd have stopped him. However, I was crying so hard that my eyes were dimmed and my voice was choked up. What he said made me hide my face in my pillows and cry out loud. He'd sworn not to leave me, blind as I was! He'd keep me in his heart like a sufferer's pain! I don't want so much good fortune, but the heart is selfish.

After the first forceful flood of tears stopped, I drew his dear face to my breast and wept, "Oh, Love, why did you swear so big an oath? I didn't ask you to remarry for happiness. I asked you to remarry for selfish reasons. I'd have seen to my own interest when the second wife came, because I can't do my work and yours alone. The parts I can't take care of because I'm blind I'd have made her do."

"Even maid servants work," my husband said, "But can I make myself marry a maid servant and put her on the same pedestal as this mine goddess?" So saying he lifted my face and kissed me between the eyebrows. That sweet, pure kiss seemed to open up my inner eye, and right then I became as a goddess; I felt that this was all for the better and told myself so. As I'm blind and cannot be a normal housewife, I shall as a goddess do good to my husband. I'd have no more lies or deception and cast away the pettiness of the common housewife.

All that day, I had to struggle with myself. The thought that my husband could not remarry lest he break his solemn oath thrilled me with an almost unbearable pleasure. As hard as I tried, I couldn't let go of it. The new goddess that had entered into my being today said, 'the day may come when remarriage would be better than keeping this oath,' the old woman in me countered, 'be that as it may, but he's sworn not to, so he can't.' the goddess said, 'well, whatever may be the case, you shouldn't be so pleased.' The woman said, "I understand, but when he's sworn . . ." etc., etc. The words were repeated over and over. The goddess only grimaced in silence then and the darkness of a dire prediction shrouded my heart.

My repentant husband forbade all the servants and attempted to take over all my chores along with his other responsibilities. This helpless dependence on him in even minor matters was very pleasant at first, for that way I could always have him near. Because I could not see him with my eyes, the desire to have him always beside me grew poignantly ardent. The part that my eyes had had when they could see my husband was now taken over by the other senses, which divided that part between them. Now, if my husband were away for any length of time, I felt I was floating on air with nothing to hold on to, and as if I had lost everything. Before, when my husband would leave for college, I would open the gable window a chink and watch the carriage take him away. If he were late home, I'd stand at the window and wait for him. I'd tied his world to mine with what I could see. Now my whole blind body seeks him and longs for him. The bridge between his world and mine is now broken. Now only this impenetrable blindness separates him and me; all I can do is to wait helplessly for him to come home. So nowadays, whenever he comes home after even a brief absence, my whole being rushes to embrace him, and my heart cries out for him.

But so much ardent desire, such dependence can bode only ill. For one thing, the burden of a wife on her husband is heavy enough; I could not make it heavier by imposing my blindness on him too. Let me endure my ever-darkened world by myself. I promised wholeheartedly not to tie my husband to me by my eternal blindness.

In a short while I trained myself to function by touch, smell and sound. I could even do some daily chores better than I had before. I thought now that sight hinders us from doing our chores more than it helps. The eyes see far more than is necessary, and when the eyes guard one, the ears get blunted and lazy, hearing less than they should. Now that the eyes were not there, my other senses began doing their work far better.

Now I did not let my husband do any of my work for me, doing it myself as I had before.

"Why are you keeping me from my expiation?" asked my husband.

"I know not what you need to expiate," I replied, "But why sin any more than I already have?"

Whatever he said aloud, I could sense my husband's sigh of relief when I released him from his unease. No man should make it his vocation to care for a blind wife all life long.

After qualifying as a physician, my husband took me to the suburbs.

I came to the village as back to my mother's lap. I'd left the village at eight, very soon after I was married. Now it's ten years later; my birthplace had dimmed like a mere shadow in my memory in the meantime. The city of Calcutta obscured my senses as long as I could see around me. Today, with my sight gone, I realize that Calcutta is a city that charms only the eye, and fails to touch the heart. As soon as my sight was gone, the village of my childhood rose shining as brightly as a starry night in my mind's eye.

We went to Hashimpur at the beginning of December. The country around was new to me. I had no idea how it looked; but the feelings and the smells of my childhood wrapped lovingly about me. That sweet morning breeze blowing over dew-moistened, just harrowed grain-fields, that all-pervading sweet spiciness of mustard and urad fields, the shepherd boy singing his pensive melodious lays, and even the rattling of the oxcart-wheel as it rolled by thrilled me with pleasure. Those memories from my early childhood focused sharper now, all the better because my blind eyes had lost their power of contradiction. I went back to my childhood days, but could not find Ma. In imagination I saw Gran with her few remaining hairs open and with her back to the sun, making daal vadis, but her faint trembling voice singing the spiritual songs she loved was missing. That yearly feast of thanksgiving rose clear in the dewy skies of winter, but where among the groaning sound of the husking pedal threshing new rice were the voices of my little girlfriends? In the evening the sound of a cow mooing in the distance reminds me of Ma going to the barn with a taper to light the lamps; with that mingles the smell of fresh feed & smoke from burning hay and I hear the altar-bells from the neighbors' home across the pond. Someone has filtered out the material things from my childhood and left only the memories, like feelings and aromas.

Along with this my childhood ritual of worshiping Shiva every morning, offering fresh-picked flowers came back to my mind crystal clear. I have to own up that in all the hustle and bust of daily life in Calcutta, our brains seem to go a little awry. Religious observances and reverence are not accorded the wholehearted purity that they require. I remember with crystalline clarity that afternoon when a village-dwelling friend of mine came to visit me in my Calcutta home and asked, "Kumu dear, does this not anger thee? If this were to happen to me, I'd never set eyes on such a husband ever again."

Said I, "My dear, I've stopped seeing his face long ago. I'm angry at my eyes for that; why should I be angry at my husband?"

Labanya was on fire with anger at my husband for not calling the doctor on time, and she tried to make me angry too. I explained to her that living together in the world, we have to endure slings and arrows of outrageous fortune, some we are born with, some we achieve and others that are thrust at us, but if we have a steady reverence in our hearts, we achieve an inner peace despite our troubles. Otherwise life becomes a web of misgivings, misunderstanding and discontent. I am sorry enough to be blind; why increase the melancholy by heaping blame on my husband?

Needless to say, these words from a mere girl like me did not please Labanya. Angrily she shook her head and stomped off.

But whatever I say, words can hurt; they don't all go west. The angry words Labanya had uttered had left a few sparks, which I'd tried to stamp out. However, the scars remained. There are so many arguments, such talk in Calcutta! There, the mind matures precociously.

In the village the cool fragrance of the shiuli blossoms I'd offered to Shiva when I was a child enveloped me, reviving all the hope and confidence I'd taken with me to the city. The deity filled my heart and all my surroundings. I bowed low, saying, "O Lord, it's nothing to lose mine eyes when I have thee with me."

Alas, how I had misspoken! Thou art here with me is also a vain statement. I have only the right to say that I am here for thee. O my dear, one day fate will wrench these words out of me. I've no power over anyone but myself.

Some time elapsed quite pleasantly. My husband's reputation as a doctor began to spread, and we managed to save some money, too.

But money bodes no good. It suppresses the mind and all the finer qualities of human nature. When the mind reigns it can create its own happiness and enjoyment; it is only when money reigns the mind goes idle, and the simple pleasures of yesterday no longer suffice. Material things and the connotations thereof take the arrangement over.

I cannot pinpoint one particular topic or incident, but perhaps because the blind feel more, or due to whatever other reason, I felt my husband's nature change bit by bit as our situation changed. The altruistic feelings about religion, ethics and the right thing to do with which my husband had begun his career all those years ago seemed to be gradually going numb. I remember his saying, "I'm studying medicine not only for myself, but also for the common man, whom I hope to help." He detested those doctors who refused to treat dying patients without being paid first, so much so that he could hardly speak of them without choking up in hate. I realize that those days are long gone. He brushed aside the poor woman who clasped his feet and implored him to save the life of her only son; at last I had to swear upon my love to send him there. His mind, however, was elsewhere and his treatment came to naught. I know how he regarded money dishonestly earned when we had but little of it. But now we have a sizable bank balance, and a rich man's bureaucrat came two days in a row to speak secretly to him; what they discussed I have no inkling of, but when he came to me later that night and spoke brightly on sundry topics, I knew by the touch of my mind that he had sullied himself.

Where, O where is that husband of mine whom I had last beheld before blindness darkened my sight! What have I done for him who had kissed the space between mine sightless eyes and called me his goddess? Those who are felled suddenly by a storm of sin in one day can rise again by another emotion, but this gradual hardening day by day and moment by moment within oneself, expanding outwardly while being crushed inwardly, has absolutely no remedy, at least in the way I look at it.

The way my physical blindness has separated me from my husband is nothing. But oh, how mine heart grows weary when I think that he is not where I am. I, the blind woman, am still in my inner world devoid of physical light with my first youthful love, unbroken faith and total devotion—the dew hasn't dried from the flowers I offered my deity in the beginning of life with my girlish hands. And now, here my husband is, off who knows where in search of filthy lucre! The things I believe in, the things I know to be right, that I regard as richer than all other wealth in the world, he ridicules from afar. But it was not always like this; in the beginning we had started out together. Then, I know not when or where, our paths began to diverge. It has become so that when I call him today, there is no answer.

From time to time the thought has crossed my mind is that perhaps I make mountains out of molehills because I'm blind. If I could see with my eyes, I would know the world as it really is.

But all day food tasted flat to me. Waking up from his afternoon nap my husband said, "Why so miserable, my darling?"

Before, I'd have answered, "There's nothing wrong;" but the time for deception is past, so I spoke up, "I've wanted to clear things up for a long time; but I've been at a loss about what to say. I don't know if I can explain properly what I've got to say; but I'm sure you too feel that we are not where we started out. Our paths have diverged."

"Change is the norm," laughed my husband.

"Money and youth are transitory," I retorted, "but is there nothing constant in life?"

My husband grew serious, saying, "You see, my dear, other women sigh for real things, like for instance, some husbands don't earn; yet others don't love their wives. Your wants, on the other hand, are totally imaginary."

Right then I understood that my blindness had served to distance us, so much so that perhaps my husband would never understand me again.

In the meantime an aunt-in-law of mine came from her village home to see her nephew and me. When we both got up from kissing her feet, she spoke thus, "I say, Kumu dear, Destiny has made you lose your eyes. So how is our Abinash going to run his home with a blind wife? Make him take a second wife."

If my husband had laughed it away as a joke, "All right, Auntie, find one for me," it would have cleared the air up fine. But he was discomfited, "Oh Auntie, what are you saying?"

"Why, did I say anything wrong?" persisted Auntie, "Well, Kumu dear, you tell him."

"Oh Auntie, what a person to ask! Do you ask the person you're going to hurt?"

"You're very right, of course, my girl," Auntie agreed, "So, my dear Abinash, thou and I'll discuss this? What dost thou say? But I say again, Kumu dear, the more wives a well-born man has the better it is. If our boy had married without choosing to practice medicine, he'd never have wanted for money. The patient is sure to die when treated by a doctor, and dead people don't pay, but God has cursed a well-born man's wife with almost everlasting life, and the longer she lives the better for her husband it is."

A day or two later, my husband asked Auntie right in front of me, "Auntie, can you find a woman who would take care of Kumu like a sister? She can't see, and I'd be much easier in my mind if she had someone always with her." These words would have fit when I'd been newly blinded, but how my blindness hinders others or me just now I've no idea. However, I kept mum.

Auntie replied, "There is no dearth. My brother-in-law has a beautiful and talented daughter. She is of age, but for want of a suitable bridegroom she still waits to be married. If thou art the bridegroom, she'd marry thee in a trice."

Starting up, my husband said, "Who's talking about marriage?"

Auntie said then, "Just listen to thyself! Would a gentlewoman come live with thee without marrying thee?" This was very true, and my husband could not protest.

Through the eternal darkness of my blinded eyes, I faced Heavenward, imploring, "Please God, save my husband."

A few days after this, when I came out of my prayer-room, Auntie said, "Kumu dear, Hemangini, the niece I told you of, has arrived . . . . Himu my girl, this is your elder sister; kiss her feet."

In the meantime my husband came in unexpectedly and, seeing a strange woman, made as if to go out again. "Hi, Abinash my boy, where art thou off to?" Auntie asked.

"Who is this lady?" asked my husband.

"This is that niece of mine I told thee of, Hemangini," replied Auntie. When, how and indeed why this young girl was brought there, was a subject of infinite and unnecessary amazement to my husband.

I said to myself, "I understand all that's going on, but then did deception have to top it? Concealment, hiding, lies! If you want to be irreligious, then be it, but why sink so low, just to deceive me?"

Taking Hema's hand, I led her to our bedroom; I touched her all over to see her. She probably had a pretty face, and was no less than fourteen or fifteen.

The girl laughed a high, sweet laugh, "What on earth are you doing? Do you want to exorcise me?"

That free and easy laughter served to dispel the cloud between us. Putting my right hand around her neck I said, "I am looking at you, my dear."

"Looking at me?" laughed the girl again, "Am I a bean or an eggplant in your garden that you have to feel me to find out how big I've grown?"

Then I suddenly remembered that Hema did not know I'm blind. I said, "You see, sister dear, I'm blind." She was quiet and seriously amazed for some time. I felt her curious, attentive observation of me; then she said, "Oh, so that's why you've brought Anni here?"

I said, "No, I hadn't sent for her; your anni came of her own accord."

The girl laughed again, saying, "Out of love? Then this loving one is not going to move from here soon. But why did my father send me here?"

Now Auntie came in. She'd been outside, talking to my husband. As soon as she came in, Hema asked, "Anni, when are we going home?"

Auntie exclaimed, "You just got here, honey. You can't really leave this soon! I declare, I've never seen anyone so agitated."

Hema said, "Anni dear, I don't think you're here for a short visit. Well, these are your relatives, so you may stay as long as you please. But I tell you, I'm leaving as soon as possible." She took my hand then, saying,

"What do you say, dear? You are not that close to me, I believe." Not replying to all these questions from her I just drew her close. I noticed that however mighty Auntie was she could not control this young damsel. Loath to displaying anger in public, Auntie tried to show Hema a little affection; she on her part shook it off like water off a duck's back. Auntie tried to laugh it off as the pouting of a petted girl and walk away. Pausing, she said, "Himu dear, go bathe; it's time." She came to me and said, "Come, my sister, let's go bathe together." Unwillingly, Auntie gave up; she realized that Hema would win if there was a tug-of-war and the discord between them would be discourteously revealed to me.

On our way to the pond in back of our house, Hema asked me, "Why haven't you any children?"

I smiled slightly and answered, "God hasn't given me them, that's all."

"You must have had some sins inside," she rejoined.

"That also, only the Lord knows," I answered.

As proof, Hema continued, "See, Anni's mind is so crooked that she can never conceive children." I don't understand the inner meaning of sin & expiation, joys and sorrows, brickbats and bouquets. So I just heaved a long sigh and said to Him in my mind, "Only Thou knowest!" Hema laughed and hugged me, saying, "Oh, hi! You sigh even at my words? Nobody ever listens to me, you know!"

I saw that my husband was hindered in his medical practice. When a call came in from far away, he would decline it now; even a call close to home he would hurry through. Before, he would just come in for lunch and a nap when he stayed home between calls. Now, Auntie called him at odd times, as would he himself keep appearing unexpectedly. When Auntie called loudly, "Himu dear, would you bring my betel-pot?" I knew that my husband had gone to her room. For a few days in the beginning, Hema would take over the betel pot, the oil bottle, the container of vermilion etc. as required; but then she too seemed reluctant, preferring instead to stay with me and sending the required article via the maid. Auntie would call, "Hemangini, Himu, Oh Himi darling!" The young maiden would then clasp me as if in an outpouring of sympathy. An apprehension and sadness seemed to overpower her, and after this she never mentioned my husband to me.

In the meantime Dada came to see us. I knew that nothing would escape his sharp eyes, and that it would be almost impossible to hide anything from him. He is a strict judge, not letting even the most venial shortcoming off the hook. The thing I feared most was that my husband would be guilty in his eyes. I tried to cover up by being extra cheerful: by talking too much and too loudly, by pretending to be too busy, by making a big to-do, I tried to hide everything. But this was so unusual for me that it led to my almost being caught. However, Dada could stay no longer than a few days. My husband was so agitated it bordered on rudeness. Dada left; before he went away, he placed his hand on my head and silently blessed me for a long time; I understood what he wished for me. His tears fell on my tear-stained cheeks.

I remember that it was a market-day in early April. In the gathering dusk people were returning home after a busy day of trading; There had been a storm a short distance off, and the wet wind brought forth the smell of the rain-washed earth, filling the whole atmosphere; friends who had been separated called to each other eagerly. As long as I am alone in the bedroom the lamps are not lit, because of the risk of fire. I was sitting in that dark room calling silently to the Supreme Lord of this my endless blind world.

I was saying, "Me Lord, when I don't feel Thy power, when I don't understand Thy will, I grasp at the mast of this orphaned broken heart with all the strength I have; my chest is lacerated and bleeding, but contain this tempest I cannot. How far more wilt Thou test me? My strength is almost spent," So saying, my tears flowed; I laid my head on the headboard and wept. I'm so busy with housework all day. Hema shadows me all the time, so I haven't the privacy of weeping the heavy burden of tears and sadness that weighs my heart down away. After a long time today my tears wouldn't be held back any longer. In the meantime I felt the bed shake, the rustle of a person moving was heard, and just minutes later Hema came up to me and, drawing me near, began wiping my tears away gently. I don't know when she had come in to lie down on the bed. She asked no questions, nor did I tell her anything. Rather, she just stroked my forehead lovingly with her cool hands. In the meantime, I did not realize when a bad rainstorm with thunder and lightning passed overhead; after a very long time sweet peace cooled my fevered heart.

The following day, Hema said, "Anni, if you don't go home, I'm going with my Kaivarta dada, I tell you." Auntie replied, "There's no need for that, dear. I'm leaving tomorrow, too, so we can go together. See, Himu, what a beautiful pearl ring our Abinash has bought for thee," and proudly she handed the ring to Hemangini. Hemangini said, "Look, Anni, how well I can aim," and taking careful aim, threw the ring right into the pond in back of the house. Auntie had goose bumps in anger and amazement; taking my hand she implored, "Kumu dear, please don't tell Abinash about this childishness. If you love me, please, dearie!"

"You don't have to say any more, Auntie," I reassured her, "I won't tell anybody anything."

The next day, before leaving, Hema hugged me and said, "Didi dear, please remember me." Stroking her face over and over with both hands, I replied, "The blind never forget anything, sister dear; I have no visible world. So all I can live with are my memories." I drew her head to my breast and kissed it as the faint scent of freshly washed hair wafted to my nostrils. My tears fell thick and fast onto her hair.

When Hema said goodbye, my world dried up—the soft fragrance and beautiful music of friendship that she had brought me, the radiant glow and crisp freshness of real affection with which she treated me all went away with her and made me grope to find what there was all around me. My husband came in and, trying to be especially cheerful, said, "Good; now that they've left, we can get some real work done." Fie, fie on me! Why so much trickery for me? Am I afraid to face the truth? Have I ever feared pain? Didn't my husband know? When I was forced to give my sight up, did I not accept my eternal darkness placidly?

So far, only my blindness had separated me from my husband; from this day onward the curtain of subterfuge fell between us, too. Not even by mistake did my husband mention Hema to me now, as if she had vanished without a trace from the face of the earth without touching our lives in the least. However, he did get news of her through correspondence; I could feel it. Just as floodwaters entering the pond pull at the lotus-stems, news of Hema tugged at my husband's heart; and when it did, I'd feel the ripples too. When he got news of Hema, and when he did not, I was acutely aware of. However, I could not ask him about her either. I was agog for news of the bright star that had lit up my dark heart for just a brief moment and to talk openly about her, but my husband had robbed me of that privilege. She was between us like a painful, eloquent silence.

One morning at the beginning of May the maid came up to me and asked, "Mum, the big boat is being prepared with great pomp and splendor. Is the master off on a special trip?" I knew that something big was afoot; the signs of deep trouble had been intensifying on my horizon for a long while. I understood that Shankar the Destroyer had been gathering his annihilating forces atop my head all this time. "Why, I've received no news of that," I told the maid. She left with a big sigh, not daring to ask more.

Late at night, my husband came to me and said, "I have been called away to a distant place; I have to leave very early tomorrow morning, and it may be three or four days until I get back . . ."

Getting up out of bed, I asked, "Why are you lying to me?"

In a trembling, almost indistinct voice my husband asked, "What am I lying about?"

I said, "You are going to remarry!"

He was silent. I too stood stock-still. For a long time there was no sound in the room. At last I said, "Say something to answer me. Say, 'Yes, I'm going to remarry.'"

Like an echo he repeated, "Yes, I'm going to remarry."

"No, you can't go," I protested, "I shall save you from this great danger and heinous sin. If I can't save you from harm, what wife am I? What then did I worship Shiva all those years for?"

Then again the room fell silent for a long while. Lying full-length down on the ground, I clasped my husband's feet and asked, "What have I ever done to hurt you? What mistake have I made? What would you need another wife for? Please tell me, I can't stand the suspense any longer."

Then my husband said slowly, "I'll tell you the truth, I'm afraid of you. Your blindness has shrouded you in an endless veil, which I cannot draw or push aside to enter. You are my goddess, nay, more terrible than she; I cannot carry on mundane chores with you. I want a woman whom I can scold, fight with, love and make jewelery for."

"Cut my chest open and look! I am just a woman, at heart no more than the child-bride you first married; I want to trust, to depend and to worship; don't humiliate yourself to make me larger than life and hurt me more than I can bear—keep me subordinate to you in all walks of life."

I don't remember all I said. Can the angry ocean hear his own roars? I only remember saying, "If I am a pure-hearted woman, then as God Himself is my witness you cannot go back on your oath. Before that heinous sin either I shall be a widow or else Hemangini will not live," so saying I fell swooning at his feet.

When I woke up out of unconsciousness, the morning birdcalls had not yet begun and my husband had left.

I shut the door to my temple-chamber and sat in worship. I did not come out all day. In the evening a sudden nor'wester made the building quake. I did not say, "O Lord, my husband is on the river this evening; please save him." I only said eagerly, "Lord, let befall for me what may; save my husband from this grievous sin." The entire night passed; I did not leave my seat all the next day, either. Sleepless, famished, I know not who bestowed on me that superhuman strength. I sat in front of the stone idol like a stone statue myself.

In the evening, people began to knock on my door. When they succeeded in breaking down the door to enter, I had swooned and was lying unconscious.

Regaining my senses, I heard, "Didi!" I found myself lying on Hema's lap. When she shifted position a bit her very new silk sari swished. O my Lord, Thou didst not heed my prayers. My dear husband has fallen.

Lowering her head, Hema said slowly, "Didi, I've come to ask your blessing."

I seemed to have turned into wood for a moment; shaking it off a moment later, I sat up to say, "Why wouldn't I bless you, sister dear? What is your fault?"

Hema laughed her sweet high laughter, "Fault? It's no fault when you get married, and it is when I do?"

Holding Hema close, I laughed too, saying to myself, "Is what I pray for the be-all and end-all of the world? Is His will not the ultimate word? Let the sword fall on my head, but where religion and truth reside in my heart's core, I won't let anything be tarnished. I will be as I've always been. Hema bent down and kissed my feet; I blessed her, "May you always be fortunate and happy."

Said Hema, "Not only this blessing, either, but you've also to welcome your brother- in- law to your home with your dear precious hands; you can't be embarrassed." So, may I bring him in?"

"Yes," I agreed, "You may."

In a while, new footsteps entered my room and a loving voice asked, "Kumu dear, art thou well?"

"Dada!" I said in surprise, leaving my bed to kiss his feet.

"What Dada? He's your younger brother- in- law, so you can tweak his ears if you want," said Hema.

Then I understood everything. I knew that Dada had vowed never to get married; our mother had passed away long ago. We had no sister either, so there was really no one to implore Dada to tie the knot; now I'm the one who mediated in his marriage. I burst into tears, which seemed not to want to stop. Dada stroked my hair slowly, as he had so often. Hugging me, Hema only sparkled with happy laughter.

At night, sleep eluded me. With beating heart I waited for my husband, not able to decide how he would alleviate his shame and despair.

Very late at night, the door creaked open slowly. I sat up, hearing my husband's footsteps. My heart beat hard against my rib cage.

He came onto the bed and took my hand, "Darling, your dada saved me. I was about to give in to a momentary infatuation. When I got into the boat that night, only the Lord knows how heavy my heart was; on the river during the storm, I feared for my life yet wanted to drown, too, to save myself. Arriving at Mathurganj, I heard that your dada and Hema were married the night before. I cannot recount the happy embarrassment I returned to the boat in. These few days have shown me that I cannot be happy any where without you. You, my dear heart, are my goddess."

Laughing, I countered, "Please no, not a goddess; I am your wife, and only a mortal woman at that."

"Right then," retorted my husband, "You have to honor the word that you won't embarrass me by calling me your lord."

The next day, alleluias and the notes from the conch-shell filled the air of the neighborhood. Hema teased my husband non-stop, day and night. But where he'd been and what had happened there, no one mentioned.

5 THE FOUNDLING
(ORIGINAL: MALYADAAN)

This story teaches us that true and sincere love is not a thing to be trifled with, nor is a human heart a plaything.

THE MORNING HAD been rather chilly; towards noon, however, a south breeze began to blow, warming things up nicely. From the verandah where Jateen sat he could see glimpses of the now-fallow rice-field parching in the Phalgun sunshine between a gnarled old jack fruit tree with young fruit on its branches on the left and a slender, silver-barked sandpaper tree with its star-like, fragrant white blossoms on the right. On the edge of it ran a dirt road—where an oxcart rattled slowly along towards the nearby village. The thirty-something driver, with his red-and-green striped scarf around his head like a turban, sang a slow, sleepy song.

Suddenly the laughing voice of a woman called out from behind, "Hey there, Jateen! Thinking of someone from a former life?"

"Why—why Patal!" Retorted Jateen, pretending to be shocked, "Do I happen to be so out of luck that I have to draw on a former life whenever I have time to ponder?"

This woman known to her friends and relatives as Patal now said, "You don't have to be so high and mighty. I know everything there is to know about you. Fie on you, grown so old and yet you can't find a simple wife! Even our gardener, Dhana, has a wife—with whom he quarrels twice a day to let everyone know that he has indeed got a wife; and here you sit, staring out at that field and pretending to think about some pretty face—you think I can't catch on, but this is just for show. You see, Jateen, a familiar person needs no introduction. Our Dhana would never stare at the field like that even under pain of separation; even on his saddest day I've seen him hoe in hand under the mango trees, but his eyes were not so glazed over. And you, sir, who hasn't seen a wife yet and spent your time studying and dissecting dead bodies, have no need to stand and stare at the sky in the middle of the day—with a strangely murky stare. No, no, this is very shabby and irritating conduct."

Palms together, Jateen pleaded, "All right already! Please don't shame me anymore. Your Dhana is really great—I'll try to follow his example. Say no more. The first girl I see tomorrow morning shall be my wife; I can't take your insults any more!"

Patal: You promise?

Jateen: Yes, I do.

Patal: Well, then, come on!

Jateen: But where to, for goodness'sake?

Patal: Don't talk! Just come on, please!

Jateen: No, no, now you're being naughty again. I shan't go anywhere.

Patal: Okay, okay, wait here then;—and she hurried off someplace.

Let us introduce these two. Patal was only a day older than Jateen. Their fathers had been brothers, so they were first cousins as well as playmates since childhood. Because she was the older, Patal demanded certain social privileges which Jateen was reluctant to give, and for which she had complained a lot to her father and uncle when she had been younger; and so, even to the only younger brother she had, she was only Patal.

Patal was round as an orange, plump as a pumpkin and jolly as a joker. Her jolly nature spread sunshine around her everywhere. There was no power anywhere on earth that could curb her sunny, happy nature. She had just one shortcoming, if so it may be termed—she could not stand seeing sadness or tears around her. She could never be serious, even in front of her in-laws; when she had come home a preteen bride, people had talked about it. But then they saw that this was her nature and that nothing could be done about it, & gave up. Then it became so that her elders found it nearly impossible to be solemn when she was near, so sanguine was her personality. Patal could not tolerate any anxiety or long faces around her; as such the air around her sparked with conversation, laughter and yes, even a joke or two.

Patal's husband, Harakumar, was a deputy magistrate—recently transferred to the Export-tax Division in Calcutta from his regional office in Bihar. For fear of the plague, he had rented a garden-home at Bali. Because he had to go out of town often on inspections, he was seriously considering bringing his mother and a few other older female relatives to live with Patal, when young Jateen, newly-graduated from medical school and not earning money yet, came to spend a week's leave with his cousin and her family at her invitation.

On this his first day among the shady trees away from Calcutta lanes, Jateen was sitting on the shady, empty verandah rather intoxicated by the midday sun of Phalgun, when the aforementioned annoyance began. When the black-and-white patterned edge of Patal's leaf-green cotton sari had disappeared behind the filmy drapes, he relaxed for a while and settled himself more comfortably in the cushioned wicker wing-chair Harakumar had provided—his mind roaming the fairy-tale lanes of childhood at the mention of the chip-girl who was really a princess.

He had fallen into a reverie when Patal's laughing voice startled him again.

Fairly dragging another, younger girl by the hand, Patal placed her squarely in front of Jateen, asking, "Oh, Kurani dear?"

"Yes, Didi?" enquired the other girl, her voice soft and sweet.

Patal: Look and see how you like this brother of mine.

The younger girl scrutinized Jateen without any embarrassment whatsoever. Asked Patal again, "See, my dear, isn't he good-looking?"

"Mm—yes, he is," replied the girl quietly after careful consideration.

Flushing beet-red, Jateen quitted the bed, "Oh Patal, now you are being so childish!"

Patal: I am a child, and you are so very ancient! Really, people would mistake you as being years older than me.

Jateen had no other recourse but to flee. Running after him, Patal called, "Jateen, you don't have to run scared. You've got time enough to accept—there is no auspicious moment in Phalgun and Chaitra."

The damsel whom Patal called Kurani stared in astonishment. She was an olive-skinned, slim young lady of about sixteen—nothing much can be said about her face except that it was so exquisitely innocent as to remind one of a wild doe. In rough language people might call it idiocy, but it was far from stupidity. Rather, it was undeveloped intelligence, which instead of spoiling Kurani's beauty, infused it rather with a special comeliness.

Returning from Calcutta in the early evening and meeting Jateen, Harakumar exclaimed, "Ah, my dear Jateen, here you are! It's great to see you. We have a patient for you to see. While we were in Bihar during the famine, Patal and I took a maiden in to raise—Patal calls her Kurani. She and her parents were lying under a magnolia tree in front of our bungalow. When we heard the news and went, we saw that her parents had already died and that she herself, barely ten years old at the time, was fighting for life. Patal took great care to save her and nurse her back to health. No one knows what caste she is—if anybody raises a question Patal answers, 'She is twice-born; she died once and was reborn into our family. Her former caste's been washed clean off.' At first the girl started calling Patal 'Ma,' but Patal scolded, 'Don't call me Ma; call me Didi instead, alright?' Patal says, 'If such a great girl calls me Ma I'll feel so old.' Perhaps because of starvation during that famine or something else she sometimes has a painful acid stomach. Will you please examine her and find out what's wrong? . . . . Hey there, Tulsi! go get Kurani, wilt thou?"

Kurani was braiding her long, silky dark tresses as she came in and fixed her big beautiful doe-eyes of hers on both men's faces like a timid fawn.

Seeing that Jateen was hesitating, Harakumar said to him, "No need to hesitate, my dear Jateen. She only looks big; she is as immature as a green coconut, with only juice and no copra inside. She doesn't understand anything. Don't mistake her for a woman; she is a wild doe."

Jateen went ahead with a check-up; Kurani was not embarrassed in the least. "As far as I can see, there is nothing physically wrong with her," said Jateen.

"Neither is anything wrong with her heart; want to see an example?" quipped Patal, suddenly coming in. Going to Kurani, she lifted the younger woman's comely pointed chin in both her hands, asking, "Kurani dear, do you like this brother of mine?"

"Yes," Kurani nodded.

"Want to marry him?"

"Yes," nodded Kurani once more, this time smiling a little. When Patal and Harakumar started to laugh, Kurani joined in, not understanding the joke one little bit.

Blushing rose pink, Jateen said, "Oh Patal, now you've really gone too far—how wrong! Harakumarbabu, you indulge Patal far too much for my liking."

"Then neither can I expect her to indulge me," responded Harakumar, "but Jateen, you've worked yourself up to such a frenzy simply because you don't know Kurani as well as Patal and I do. By blushing you'll teach even Kurani to blush, I see. Everybody makes fun of her—don't spoil it by being so dead serious."

Patal: This is just why Jateen and I have been so at odds over the years. My God! He's so serious.

Harakumar: So you learned to quarrel—now that your brother's gone off, you . . . .

Patal: There you go, lying again! It's no fun picking a quarrel with you, so I don't even try.

Harakumar: I give up before we even start being interesting.

Patal: What a thing to do! If you went on until the end, things would be so much better.

That night, as the unclouded harvest moon shone in through the open east window, Jateen opened the other window and the two doors to his room and sat deep in thought in the cushioned armchair Harakumar had provided. This young maid, who had watched her parents slowly and painfully succumb to starvation and been so near death herself has such a grievous shadow cast over her whole life. Having grown up with this deep pain inside her, was she to be made fun of? What seemed pure fun to Patal and her husband must hurt poor Kurani a lot. The Good Lord has mercifully veiled her senses in forgetfulness—if that veil were to be lifted, the dire cruelty of the world around her would be exposed. This noon hour, while Jateen sat pensively watching the sky between the sandpaper tree and the jack fruit tree, the soft, drifting aroma of jack fruit-blossoms slowly blended into the soft southerly breeze, lulling his olfactory nerves to observe the world through rose-tinted lenses; that simple girl with her big black doe-eyes shredded that myth to bits. The real, everyday world concealed behind this fresh, beautiful Spring day—standing so enormous suffering hunger and thirst—became apparent behind the sweet artistic ivory-white drapes with curling green vines drawn on them.

The next evening, just after sunset, Kurani suffered that threatening pain of hers. Patal hurriedly sent for Jateen; when he came in, he saw a very stiff Kurani having convulsions. She was sweating, and her face had begun to turn blue. Jateen sent a servant out for some antacid tablets and ordered a hot water bottle.

"O my Lord, see the big doctor! Her soles are frigid—why not rub some hot oil into them?" advised Patal.

Jateen began to rub hot oil forcefully into the soles of his patient's feet. This took quite a while; it grew very late. Back from work in Calcutta, Harakumar came in repeatedly to inquire after Kurani. He was at his wits' end without Patal, Jateen understood—and thus these frequent inquiries.

"Harakumarbabu needs you desperately," implored Jateen, "Please do go to him, Patal."

"That's right, talk of others indeed!" Flashed Patal, "I know very well who the impatient one happens to be. What a relief it would be for you if I went now! And here you blush at every word—I'd no inkling things had gone this far!"

Jateen: All right already! Stay here, then. Oh dear Lord, I'd be relieved to see and hear you shut up for once. I misunderstood—maybe Harakumarbabu is at peace. He doesn't get this kind of opportunity often."

When Kurani opened her eyes in relief, Patal remarked, "Thy husband strove and implored long and hard to bring thee back tonight, and thou art this late! Fie on thee! Go kiss his feet."

Kurani dutifully kissed Jateen's feet right then and there; Jateen hurried from the room.

From the next day, a volcano of bother exploded on Jateen. At lunch, just as he had taken his first bite of paratha and aaloo dam, Kurani came in with a hand-held, exquisitely designed woven fabric fan and began to fan the flies away.

"No, no, no need for that," Jateen frowned in agitation. Amazed at this forbidding attitude, Kurani cast a furtive glance over her shoulders at the room beyond, and resumed fanning.

"Oh Patal, "remarked Jateen to the opne behind the scene, "If you go on teasing me like this I won't eat . . . . I'm leaving now."

As Jateen pretended to leave off eating and get up, he saw Kurani's sweet simple face darken with real pain; instantly apologetic, he sat down again. Jateen had begun to believe, as Patal and Harakumar seemed to, that Kurani understood nothing and felt no pain or embarrassment; but now he saw that there are exceptions to every rule, and that no one knows when or where, or even how, these exceptions can take over. Kurani laid down the fan and left.

The next morning after breakfast, as Jateen sat on that cushioned wicker chair on the verandah reading the newspaper, the mother cuckoo sang from the jasmine arbor and the heady perfume of jasmine mingled with the tangy aroma of mango blossom—he spied Kurani, clad in a leaf-green sari with her hair in a half-braid, hesitate a bit to come out with his cup of tea. She had a timidly fearful look in her eyes—whether Jateen would be annoyed if she took him his cup was a thought that seemed to elude her. Feeling rather sorry, Jateen advanced to take the cup from her. Could this fawn in human form be hurt for so insignificant a reason? But no sooner had Jateen taken the cup than he saw Patal emerge with closed fists and a derisive smile curling her full lips as if to say, 'Now I've caught you red-handed!'

That evening after supper, as Jateen sat in his bedroom leafing through a research journal outlining new paths to follow, the familiar spicy-sweet fragrance of bakul blossoms startled him. He looked up to see Kurani entering the room with a triple string of fresh bakul in her hand.

"Oh, no! This is too much," said Jateen to himself, "We mustn't let Patal play this cruel game any more."

Said he to Kurani, "Shame on you, Kurani! Why do you go along with your didi's heartless games? Can't you see she's only playing with you to amuse herself?"

Ere he had finished, Kurani shyly and timidly made as if to go. Hurriedly calling her back, Jateen begged, "Kurani, won't you show me your garland, please?" and took it from her hand. Kurani's face lit up in pleasure like a thousand-watt light, and at that very moment, profuse high, sweet laughter, mingling the tinkle of bangles and the flow of river water, rang out from beyond the closed door of Patal's bedroom.

Going into Jateen's bedroom the next morning to tease, Patal found the room empty—Jateen wasn't there; his cheap leather suitcase, his books and journals were all gone too. On the little night-table lay a dog-eared scrap of paper with the words, "I'm running away—Shri Jateen," in his handwriting.

"Hey—oh, Kurani, thy husband's gone. Couldn't hold him, eh?" laughed Patal, affectionately tweaking Kurani's braids on her way into housework.

It took Kurani a little while to grasp the full import of what Patal had just said. Standing as rigidly still as a stone statue she stared blankly straight ahead. Then, slowly and painfully as if on leaden feet, she entered the little bedroom which Jateen had occupied. She found it empty of Jateen's things; only the string of bakul, her gift of the previous evening, lay on the little night-table.

It was a beautiful, gentle spring morning; the golden light of the sun, playing on the leaves of the Krishnachura tree, had made filigree of light and shade on the verandah. Squirrels and chipmunks scampered about with their tails in the air, searching out their hidden caches of nuts, berries and seeds, and the many different species of songbirds sang, twittered and chirped their melodious medleys, seemingly unable to stop talking. The joy of life had begun to take shape in this corner of the world with its picturesque interplay of light and shade; in the midst of all this stood that bud of a girl, uncomprehending of her surroundings and her life. Oh, it was a tough puzzle indeed! What did happen, why, how and wherefore it happened the way it did, and then why this affectionate home, these kindly folks and this beautiful golden morning suddenly became so drab and blank, she had no idea. Who was it then lowered this little damsel with no lamp in her hand into this dark chasm of suffering in her own heart? Who indeed could lift her again onto this material world, with trees full of singing birds and forests teeming with calling animals who were not aware of themselves?

After finishing her housework, Patal came looking for Kurani and found her in the room Jateen had vacated, clutching the front left leg of the four-poster bed, shaped like a lion's paw—as if begging for something from that empty place, as if, indeed, she was emptying all the sweet nectar of love in her heart at a pair of unseen feet, hoping against all hope for a miracle—this loosely clad, wild-haired woman heaped on the ground seemed to be saying in eager silence, "Take me, oh please take me, beloved mine!"

"Hey Kurani, what's going on here?" exclaimed Patal in surprise.

Kurani didn't get up; she stayed prostrate as she had been. When Patal came close and touched her, she could not keep her tears back any longer and hysterical sobs racked her slim body.

"Oh, my God, what hast thou done!" exclaimed Patal again in apprehension, "Thou silly girl, to go and fall in love indeed!"

Informing Harakumar about Kurani's state of mind, Patal asked, "You see what has happened now? Where were you, and why didn't you stop me from playing this stupid and dangerous game?"

"But what would have been the use? I don't usually try to stop you . . . . that is not my way at all," countered Harakumar lamely.

Patal: Oh, what a husband! If I do make a mistake, can't you stop me by force? Why did you let me toy with people's feelings?"

So saying, she ran over to the prostrate maiden and, clutching her neck affectionately, implored, "Tell me what thou hast to say, my sweetheart!"

But oh, had Kurani the eloquence to voice the unspoken mysteries of her heart? In her breast lay concealed an unspoken, unspeakable grief; she knew not what it was, or whether it affected others the same way it had affected her. She did not even know what it was called. She could only sob brokenheartedly to express her feelings.

"Kurani, thou hast a very naughty Didi," said Patal, near tears herself, "But she never thought thou wouldst take her words so much to heart. Nobody believes thy Didi ever; why didst thou make such a huge mistake, my dear one? Kurani, please lift thy head, look at thy Didi and tell her thou forgivest her."

But Kurani, whose heart had turned away, could in no way look at Patal; she hid her head in her hands even more forcefully. Without understanding, she was upset at Patal, who then disengaged herself and got up to go and stand near the full-length, clear-paned window through which the long slim leaves of the areca-palm tree, glimmering in their sheen of Phalgun sunlight, could be seen. The sight somehow brought tears to her eyes.

The next morning, Kurani seemed to have vanished without a trace. Patal, a rag-tag dresser herself who did not care what she had on, lavished her love of costume on Kurani, buying her nice clothes and appropriate jewelry. Those pretty clothes and jewelry, collected over a number of years, were all lying in a heap on the floor of her little bedroom. Even the pair of thin wire-wrapped bangle-bracelets that she usually wore and the little clove-shaped ornament for her nose were left behind, as if she had wanted only to shake off all her Pataldidi's affection for her off herself, and start over.

Harakumar notified the police, as he should in such cases; but though he gave an accurate description of Kurani, the police were hard-pressed to find her; because hundreds of people were fleeing the city for fear of the plague, one particular person in that milling throng proved a needle in a haystack to find. After many dead-end leads, Harakumar gave up on Kurani. She who had come into their lives out of the unknown all those years ago seemed to have vanished into it again.

After a very intense job-hunt, Jateen found a job as the attending physician at the local plague hospital. One afternoon as he came in after lunch, he heard that a new patient, whom the police had picked up off the roadside, had been admitted into the women's section.

Jateen was on call that afternoon, and he went to see her. Most of her face was hidden under the sheet. First of all Jateen took her hand to feel her pulse; she had a very low fever and was very weak. Then, putting the sheet aside to examine her, he saw that it was—yes, that's true—the same Kurani.

Meanwhile Patal and Harakumar had filled Jateen in on Kurani. Those big, beautiful doe-eyes of hers, shaded by unspoken thoughts, had intruded constantly on Jateen's mind, their gaze tearless and pained. This afternoon those same eyes, edged in the dark circles of sickness with long fans of lashes veiling wan cheeks, lay like dead weights at Jateen's breast. Why had the dear Lord, after making this little lady as sweet and delicate as a flower with great care, seemingly toss her from the famine into the plague? This gentle young soul, that lay near death in bed tonight, had endured pain beyond measure, danger beyond calling within its very brief span; and indeed, wherefore and how did Jateen end up embroiled in her affairs like a sore third dilemma? A sigh, mingled with a joyous note, beat against Jateen's breast. This rare love, that had fallen at his feet like a blossom full-blown, when he'd had no idea that it existed, had enriched his life a thousand fold. The love that comes even to death's door to gratify itself blesses him who receives it as well as her who gives it. Who on earth is worthy enough of such pure untainted love?

Sitting beside Kurani, Jateen held a glass of warm milk to her lips, encouraging her to take tiny sips. After what seemed a very long time indeed, Kurani opened her eyes with a long sigh. Looking at Jateen, she tried to recall him as one might recall a distant dream. When Jateen placed an affectionate hand on her forehead and called, "Kurani!" the last haze of her unconsciousness went away, she came fully awake and recognized him; a cloud of infatuation fell over her eyes and a saturated tenderness like the first solemn rain clouds of the season seemed to fill them.

"Come, Kurani, drink up this bit of milk, there's a dear," said Jateen as if he were urging a favorite sister.

Sitting up a little, staring fixedly at Jateen, Kurani slowly finished up that bit of milk.

Now, if a doctor at a hospital spends all his time with one patient, no work gets done; it is not good at all. So, when Jateen got up to go see other patients, Kurani's gaze became apprehensive. Taking her thin hot hand in both his own, Jateen reassured her, "Don't worry, Kurani dear! I'll be back as soon as I can."

Jateen took great pains in informing the authorities that this new patient was weak from malnutrition and not the plague at all; so if she were to stay here with other plague-patients, she might get really sick. He obtained permission from his superiors to take her elsewhere and took her to his little apartment; he wrote a detailed letter to Patal and Harakumar, explaining everything.

That evening none save the doctor and the patient were in the little bedroom Jateen had fitted up for Kurani. Near the headboard of the twin bed, a kerosene lamp covered in colored paper shed a soft shady glow, and on the bracket a little clock swung its pendulum and ticked, it seemed too loudly, in the otherwise silent room.

Touching Kurani's forehead, Jateen asked, "Well, my dear Kurani, how do you feel?"

For answer Kurani pressed his hand more firmly onto her forehead.

"Feeling better?" Questioned Jateen again.

"Yes," replied Kurani with her eyes half-closed.

"Hi, Kurani, what's this you have around your neck?" asked Jateen.

Quickly, Kurani tried to hide it under her clothes. Jateen noticed that it was a dried string of bakul. He recalled then what this string symbolized: his mind went back to the warm afternoon when this same string had been fresh. Amidst the ticking of the clock, Jateen sat silently pondering. When had Kurani the fawn grown up to be this young woman with so painful a yearning in her heart? By what heat and light had the clouds over her intellect parted to reveal the embarrassment, the deep pain she sought so carefully to conceal from the world around her?

At about 2:00 or 2:30 A. M. Jateen found himself falling asleep over his newspaper while sitting on a stool by the side of Kurani's bed. Suddenly the slow creak of the door opening startled him awake. Through the haze of sleep, he saw Patal entering with Harakumar behind her, carrying a small suitcase and a large, bulging leather shoulder-bag.

"When your letter reached us," began Harakumar, speaking to Jateen, "We decided to start after sun-up and went to bed. Around midnight Patal began to beg me to start right away; you know she doesn't take no for an answer. So we called a cab, and here we are."

"Darling, please go sleep on Jateen's bed, alright?" said Patal gently to her husband.

After demurring a little Harakumar went to bed in Jateen's room where he soon fell fast asleep.

Returning, Patal beckoned Jateen to a corner and asked, "Any hope?"

Coming over to Kurani and feeling her pulse, Jateen shook his head to indicate no hope.

Not divulging herself to Kurani, Patal took Jateen aside to ask, "Tell me, Jateen—speak the truth, now—do you love Kurani or not?"

Not replying to Patal, Jateen came to sit beside Kurani's bed and shook her, taking her hot hand, "Kurani! oh, Kurani dear!"

Kurani opened those incredibly beautiful eyes of hers and said with a flicker of a quiet, sweet smile, "Yes, Dadababu, what is it?"

"Kurani, please put this string of yours around my neck," pleaded Jateen earnestly. Kurani stared unblinkingly at him, seeming not to understand.

"Please won't you give me your string?" implored Jateen once more.

At these words from Jateen, Kurani was pained when she remembered his former disregard and neglect of her, "But Dadababu, what good will that do now?"

"It will do a lot of good," smiled Jateen, picking up Kurani's frail brown hand in both his strong ones, "Because, Kurani my sweetheart, I love you more deeply than the deepest ocean."

Hearing that confession, Kurani pondered in silence a bit, her eyes brimming over with tears. When Jateen knelt beside her bed with his head close to her hands, she took the string of dried bakul from around her own neck and put it around his.

Then Patal came to Kurani's bedside and called gently, "Kurani, Kurani darling!"

"Oh, Didi, it's you," responded Kurani weakly, her wan face brightening.

"Thou art not angry with me any more, dearest?" asked Patal, coming nearer and taking her hand.

"No, no, Didi dear, of course not," smiled Kurani, regarding her affectionately.

"Jateen, please go into your bedroom a bit," ordered Patal. When Jateen had disappeared behind the curtain, Patal opened the big bag and took out a hibiscus-red Vanarasi sari and some jewelry for Kurani. Without moving the patient much, she carefully draped the sari over Kurani's stale clothes. Putting a rose-cut bracelet on each wrist, she added a thin bangle too, and called, "Jateen, get back in here!"

When Jateen, having washed his face and combed his hair, came back, Patal handed him a rose-cut gold necklace of Kurani's. Taking it and lifting Kurani's head gently, Jateen put it around her neck.

When the morning sunlight touched Kurani's face, her spirit had already departed for the gates of heaven and she didn't see it any more. The vibrant, tranquil freshness of her face made it seem as if she hadn't died—just fallen asleep, dreaming an endless happy dream, submerged in it.

When it came time to take the body away, Patal fell crying onto Kurani's breast, and said,

"How fortunate thou art, my darling! In death thou art far happier than thou ever wert in life."

Looking at Kurani's peaceful, dead face, Jateen thought, "He Whose treasure she was has taken her back, without depriving even me."

6

THE HOUSE OF CARDS
(ORIGINAL: TASHER DESH)

In this fantasy, Tagore made all the characters except the three major ones puppets. Although it may seem like a fairy tale, this story, an allegory of India under British rule, speaks out for liberty.

PART I

ON THE FARAWAY ocean there lies an isle where only the Kings, Queens, Aces and Jacks of Cards live. There are more homesteaders, from Twos and Threes to Nines and Tens, but these happen not to be well-born.

Aces, Kings and Jacks are the principal clans; Nines and Tens are in-between, not fit to associate with them.

However, everything is in perfect order. The value and prestige of each one has been decided long ago; no one even dreams of deviating from that. Instead, each one solemnly performs the duty assigned to him—just following the grooves set down by his predecessors, like figure-skaters going through their compulsory movements. They are very afraid of change, so they have forced themselves into a groove.

What they do is very difficult for strangers to get; it might look like child's play—just moving back and forth, side by side, rising and falling according to a rigid set of rules, as if an unseen hand were pulling the strings to make them go.

With their utterly expressionless faces they look like caricatures, as they have since time immemorial. From their hats to their shoes, they have always been the same.

They have nothing to think about or ponder; they move about silently, as if lifeless. When they fall, they fall noiselessly. From below, they stare hard up at the horizon.

Their faces are very expressionless, looking blank and placid all the time like pictures. From the days of yore, everything from their shoes to their hats have been just this way.

No one nurses any desire, wishes or fears. No one tries to carve out a new path, laugh or cry; there are no doubts or hesitations. These living dead do not even flutter like birds in cages.

Once upon a very long time ago, however, these cages were home to live birds; They would sway and bird songs & flapping wings could be heard within, reminding one of the open sky and deep green forest. Now only the empty cages, reminiscent of prison-bars, are there, with no way to tell whether the birds have died or flown away.

It is a very peculiar, suffocating peace and quiet, like the calm before a storm. Complete contentment and comfort reign supreme. On the roads & streets and in the homes everything is orderly and predictable-no sound, no disagreement, no eagerness or enthusiasm¬-just small, menial everyday tasks interspersed with shorter than short rest periods.

The sea, with its waves crashing in thunderous concert, foams and spurts up to the shore and lulls the whole island to sleep. The deep blue sky spreads out over the island like the expansive wings of some protective angel-bird. From afar the blue-green horizon of a borderland can be discerned—from where no hint of discontentment can reach out to these shores.

PART II

On that faraway shore, in another land, lives a prince, with his mother the banished Queen. With his exiled mother he spends his childhood and youth doing whatever pleases him on the sandy, rocky seashore.

Sitting alone, he spins an enormous casting-net of lofty ambitions; as he flings it far and wide, he imagines himself gathering up all the unsolved mysteries of the world. His restless heart craves adventure in distant lands—especially the one whose verdant boundaries beckon to him from afar; he wants to seek out exotic plants and gems, and maybe even the secret spell to awaken the sleeping Aurora in Maleficent's tower, a princess as radiant as the sun for which she's been named, and talented beyond compare in the housewifely arts.

The Prince of course attends school in the local one-room schoolhouse, where he has the only son of the richest merchant in town and the elder son of the local police chief as his classmates. These three would always meet after class and exchange news & stories of faraway lands, and tall tales too.

When rain clouds darken the sky and it begins to pour sheets and curtains, the Prince, big though he is, sidles up to his mother at the doorstep and requests her, "Ma dear, won't you please tell me a story of faraway lands?" His mother would then begin some long-winded fairy-tale she had perhaps heard from her own mother and grandmother when she herself was a child. In the falling summer rain, the Prince's heart would yearn for sights unseen and places unvisited as he heard that twice-told tale.

One day after school the three classmates met as usual. Quoth the merchant's son to the Prince, "Dear friend, I've finished all the studying I'm ever going to do. Now I'm off to see the world, so I've come to say good-bye."

"I'll go with you," said the Prince.

"Wait just a minute!" exclaimed the policeman's son, "You're not leaving me alone here? I'm coming with you, too."

The Prince went to his poor mother and said, "Ma, I'm off traveling—you just wait, I'll find a way to alleviate your sorrows.

The three friends set off.

PART III

The merchant's fleet of twelve five-masted schooners was ready. The three friends chose the largest and grandest of these and boarded.

The white sails unfurled to the south breeze and they sailed smoothly away, like the desires in the heart of the young Prince.

From Conch Island they collected a shipload of conch-shells; Sandalwood Isle yielded a shipload of sandalwood paste. Coral Island gave our sailors a shipload of coral in its myriad hues.

The next four years brought shiploads of ivory, musk, cloves and nutmeg, before a sudden catastrophic typhoon sank all the ships. The largest and grandest ship, where the three friends were, flung them onshore, crashed against the rocks and was dashed to pieces.

It is on this island that the House of Cards: the Aces, Kings, Queens and Jacks, along with their lesser compatriots, live according to their rigid set of rules. The Tens & Nines, Twos & Threes, and others, can do no better than to follow blindly.

PART IV

In the Land of Cards there had never been an upheaval as now became slowly evident. All the Cards were very puzzled; they scratched their heads as they tried to figure out to which number the three newcomers rightly belonged: were they Aces, Queens, Kings, Jacks, Nines or Tens, and maybe even Twos or Threes? And then again, which suits were they: Spades, Hearts, Diamonds or Cloves? Unless these questions were answered, it would be almost impossible to get along with them. Where and when, and even how, they would eat or sleep, stand or sit, or even lie down, were seemingly burning questions which none seemed able to answer.

Such unease and anxiety were completely new to the Cards; however, our three newcomers were worried not a bit about these grave matters. They were starving, so they ate whatever food they could lay their hands on.

This conduct surprised even Two and Three; Quoth Three, "Oh, Two my friend, these newcomers don't differentiate."

Responded Two with gravity, "Yes, Three dear, I can easily see that these folks are lower-suited than even we are"

Having finished their meal, and rested, the Prince and his two friends observed that the people of this land were peculiar, like rootless plants yanked out of the earth; stupidly avoiding the world, they swung and swayed around. Whatever they did, seemed done by another hand, like marionettes in a puppet-show. Their faces were expressionless, betraying not even anxiety. They exercised not even the power to think for themselves. It was odd to see them moving in the groove they had carved for themselves.

Careful scrutiny of these living dead and their strictly formal goings-on made the prince lift his head heavenward and laugh out in a mixture of mirth and derision. That loud laugh of genuine amusement sounded oddly uncomfortable in the otherwise silent streets and roads of the Land of Cards. Everything here is so prim and proper, so ancient, so neat and tidy, so solemn that the sound of that loud, unrestrained laugh, startled at itself, ended as abruptly as it had begun; everything became twice as still and silent as before.

The Prince's two companions came up to him and said," Let's get out of here quick, because I'm afraid if we stay here any longer we have to pinch ourselves often to make sure we're alive!"

"No, my dear friends," the Prince stopped them, "Curiosity has killed my cat, and I want to find out if these humanoids have any life of their own."

PART V

Some time passed thus; but these three foreign youth seemed not to follow any set code of conduct, doing nothing they were seemingly supposed to do—such as rising, falling, turning the head, lying on the stomach or back, shaking heads or turning somersaults; instead they just kept looking on at these acts and breaking into trills of mirthful laughter. The solemnity of these acts seemed not to intimidate or overpower them.

One fine morning the King, Jack and Ace of Spades came over to the three friends poker-faced and asked solemnly, "Why aren't you following the rules of our Kingdom?"

"Because we don't wish to," replied the three in unison.

"Wish? Who in the world does he happen to be?" Asked the three leaders of the House of Cards in chorus. Although they did not realize it right then, by and by they started to. Gradually they understood that there was not just one way of looking at or doing things such as moving or working, that there are two sides to every story and that no one person has the right to control another. Three living examples taught them that discipline should not be so rigid as to limit man's freedom to choose. Thus was it that they gradually came to grips with the power of wishing for something so ardently that they worked to make it come true.

As soon as that power was felt, the house of cards trembled from basement to attic, like a just-awakened python slowly stretching and uncoiling itself.

PART VI

The hitherto unmoved Queens had hardly glanced at anyone. Tranquil and silent, they had gone about their allotted tasks. On this balmy Spring afternoon, however, one of them suddenly batted her long, dark fans of lashes and shot an amorous glance at the prince. It lasted just an instant, but that was enough.

"Where on earth did that come from?" thought the Prince in amazement, "I thought these were nothing but mannequins; now I realize she's a woman, and very lovely at that."

Calling the merchant's son and the policeman's son to a secluded spot, the Prince said, "My friends, this Queen has a sweetness all her own. When my eyes met her jet-black ones full of new significance, I seemed to be face-to-face with the first sunrise of a newly-formed universe. Our long, patient stay here has at last borne fruit."

Smiling, his two friends remarked curiously, "Is this true, comrade?"

From that moment on, that poor, lovesick Queen of Hearts began to get thoroughly muddled up. She would be at the wrong place at the wrong time, oftener and oftener. For instance, when she was supposed to be next to the Jack, she would go stand next to the Prince instead.

"O Queen, you've made a mistake," the poker-faced Jack would declare. The naturally-rosy cheeks of the unfortunate Queen would flush rosier at that, and she would lower her tranquil gaze.

"That was no mistake," the Prince would declaim in unseemly haste, "I've become the Jack from now on."

What unforeseen beauty, unimaginable charm and grace now emanated from the woman's heart! Her walk was sweetly agitated, her heart seemed to speak volumes through her beautiful eyes, and her whole being sent forth an offering of sweet surrender at the altar of true, vibrant love.

In correcting this new offender, the others themselves now began to make more and more mistakes. The Ace shed his habitual dignity like a snake shedding its skin. The King and the Jack became almost as one; even the Nines and Tens were no exception.

The cuckoo had heralded Spring to this isle since time immemorial; never before, though, had her songs been so significant or held so much inner meaning. The Ocean, too, had sung his monotonous monody on these shores for ages in utter disregard for anything but the dignity of Nature; now suddenly he seemed to be trying to express the agitation seething in his own heart in plays of light and shade, gestures and movements like the waves of uncontrollable youth and vivacity all over the world, unleashed by the warm South Breeze.

PART VII

Does this happen to be that same Ace, that very same King and indeed that selfsame Jack? Where have their fat, contented round faces vanished to? Now all are jittery and agitated; some look up at the sky, some laze around on the beach, some cannot sleep at night and still others seem to have lost their appetites.

On some faces envy is clearly drawn, some cast lovesick glances at the girls and women, some are fidgety and restless, a few laze around on the beach, and one or two pass sleepless nights. Some even betray apprehension and fear. At some places there is laughter and merriment, at others tears and sadness; still others reverberate to music. These people have a sudden awareness of themselves and of others. They have begun to compare themselves to each other.

The Ace, with arched neck, struts around thinking, "Hmm, the King isn't a bad-looking brat; but he's so graceless—whereas look at me, such an epitome of grace that women would fall for me in an instant."

"Oh dear, there's that chap the Ace," thinks the King, "going around with such a swelled head, as if the women are swooning over him," and regards himself in the mirror with a sardonic twist of the lips.

All the women of the land make themselves up as if their very lives depend upon it. Pointing fingers at each other, they say, "Oh, my good Lord! Look at how that vain gal is preening herself. Why does she give herself such airs? How embarrassing it is to see that go on!" and go about making themselves twice as noticed as before.

And somewhere two friends, or even yet two girlfriends, huddle naughtily over each other's secrets. Trills of giggles can be heard, and sometimes tearful sniffles come forth. Sometimes two friends stop speaking over some insignificant detail, and plead & entreat to re-establish friendship.

The youth sit nonchalantly by the roadside with their legs outspread, and with their backs to the trees, on a crisp carpet of dry brown leaves. Perchance a blue-clad maiden ventures by on that shadowy path and averts her face as she reaches that spot. As if she had no appointment to meet anyone, she passes right on by.

Observing that, some infatuated youth would perhaps approach her awkwardly, then stand there gaping and fidgeting uncomfortably for want of just the right words. The golden opportunity would slip by like sands through the hourglass, and the pretty maid would disappear round the bend.

The South Breeze, fragrant with the scent of flowers and melodious with birdcalls, would sweep over long flowing tresses and blowing sari-ends, and the unceasing roll of the sea would wave the innermost, unspoken desires of the heart.

One balmy Spring, three foreign youth raised full gale like this upon a dead sea.

PART VIII

The Prince noticed that the land seemed caught between ebb and flood tides—no speech, just taking one step forward and two backward—only heaping wishes upon cravings and desires to build and break sand-castles. It was as if they sat in their designated corners burning up by the fire of wishes and desires unfulfilled and getting skinnier & more speechless each day; only their eyes glowed with passion and unspoken words made their lips tremble like leaves in the wind.

Calling to gather everyone together, the Prince ordered, "Play music! Rejoice, everybody! The Queen of Hearts will choose her own husband tonight."

Instantly Nine and Ten tooted their flutes; Two and Three went to the horn and the clarinet. The joyous celebration that now flooded in washed off every vestige of solemnity.

Through this happy pandemonium one could hear the plaintive yet sweet music of the flute and the oboe. It imparted depth to pleasure, longing to meetings, beauty of expression to world-scenes, and tremulous loving to all hearts alike. Those who hadn't loved properly did, those who had grew nearly insensate with the joy and pleasure of it.

Crimson-clad, the Queen of Hearts had sat nearly all day in her own secret corner of the shady grove; she too was hearing the music from a distance, and her eyes were almost closed. Suddenly coming awake, she noticed the Prince sitting so close to her that his breath touched her face; right then she covered her hot, flushed face with both hands and swooned to the ground.

The Prince, on a walk by himself on the seashore, turned over and over in his mind that timid, furtive glance and that embarrassed fit.

PART IX

That evening, in the light of a thousand butter-and-incense lamps and the fragrance of masses of flowers, a harmonious concert of flutes, oboes and pipes played as a virgin Queen stood before her King, garland in hand and head bowed.

She could not put the garland where she wanted it to go, nor could she look up at him whom she desired with all her heart. The Prince himself lowered his head and the garland seemed to fall pat onto place. The court, which had been as silent as a painting, suddenly exploded into a storm of applause and cheers

A happy procession led the newlyweds to the throne, where the Prince was crowned King.

PART X

    The melancholy Queen from the land across the sea came to her son's new kingdom on a golden boat.

    The pictures have suddenly come to life—gone is the tranquil solemnity of yore. The ebb and flow of reality has come into this once pasteboard land and infused into it a new life-force. Now, instead of being a carbon copy of another, each person has his or her own personality.

7 THE LAND OF NO RETURN (ORIGINAL: CHHUTI)

In this story Tagore focuses in on an adolescent's need for love and understanding. Although they love adventure, their hearts crave love, understanding and acceptance.

A TOTALLY NEW idea for a fun game to play suddenly threw young Phatik Chakravati, leader of the neighborhood boys, into throes of agitation. On the grassy riverbank lay a thick saal log, about a foot around, waiting to be fashioned into the mast of a boat. It was this log which the boys decided to roll along.

Visualizing the annoyance and agitation of the owner of the log at not finding it exactly where and when he needed it, the other seven boys supported this naughty plan wholeheartedly.

Just as they were getting serious about starting this operation, little nine-year-old Makhanlal, Phatik's only brother, came striding up to the log and solemnly sat down on it, with a look of total disinterest very unusual for his age. The other boys were taken aback at this.

One of the boys, ten-year-old Gopal, came and tried to push Makhan off. But this little pseudo-adult would not budge. There he sat, with an expression all too serious on his little round face, seemingly contemplating the futility of all play.

"Look here, Makhan, I'll slap thee if thou dost not get off right now," scolded Phatik, his face flushing red with anger and his already shrill voice rising an octave higher—at which the little lad just changed position and remained sitting, more resolutely still.

To save face here, Phatik should immediately have slapped his disobedient brother on the cheek—but dared not. Instead he assumed an expression as if he could punish his little brother any way he chose to; of course he didn't, because he had thought up a far more amusing game. He now proposed rolling that log along, Makhan and all.

Makhan considered this a big feather in his cap. The incidental problems of such a venture, however, fazed neither him nor the others at all. The boys pushed with all their might—"Heave ho, push! Here we go, push!" The log had hardly rotated one turn when little Makhan, with all his solemn theories and serious expression, fell right to the ground.

The other lads were as pleased as Punch to have achieved such results right at the beginning of their game, but Phatik felt a twinge of unease. Makhan, meanwhile, got up, dusted himself off, and fell upon Phatik, scratching him all over the face, opening a gash on his lower lip, and hitting him blindly right and left—and ran home screaming and crying. The fun went out of playtime then, and the lads broke up.

Phatik plucked a few juicy cottonbloom stems, and sat on the bow of a half-submerged boat, absently sucking and chewing on one.

Just then, an ornate, glossily painted foreign boat dropped anchor at the dock. A middle-aged gentleman with white hair and dark moustaches disembarked and asked, "Ho there, my man! Could you point me out the Chakravarti residence?"

The youth, still tasting the sweet juice from his stem, pointed and said, "Over yonder," but as his direction was too general, the visitor had no clear idea which way to go. So he asked again, "Which way, mannie?"

"Don't know," replied the lad, and resumed sucking his stems. The visitor then sought others' help in finding his destination. No sooner had he moved on than Bagha Bagdi came up and stated, "Phatikda, Ma wants you home right now!"

"I'm not going," pouted Phatik; the stocky, very strong Bagha then picked Phatik up and carried him, kicking and screaming, all the way home.

Seeing Phatik, his mother angrily accused him, "There thou goest, hitting Makhan again!"

"But . . . but Ma, I never did," asserted Phatik.

"Lying again!"

"But I hadn't. Just ask Makhan."

When Mother asked Makhan again, he supported his earlier claim and said, "Yes, oh dear yes—he did hit me!"

Phatik could stand no more.

"What a liar!" He shouted, stepping up to Makhan and cuffing him so hard that a lump the size of a ping-pong ball appeared on the side of his head.

Mother sided with Makhan, cuffing Phatik on the back resoundingly three or four times. Phatik pushed her away and jumped back.

"Hey boy, art thou laying hands on me!" Shouted Mother.

"Hi, you all, what's going on here?" exclaimed the salt-and-pepper gentleman, now entering the little room.

In pleased surprise, Phatik's mother called out, "Oh, dear Lord, if it isn't Dada! When did you come home?" She bowed down to kiss his feet.

Dada had been working out West for quite a few years. During that time, Phatik and Makhan had been born and had grown up a bit, and Phatik's father had been killed on the job—but never once could the brother and sister find time to meet. Bishwambhar, recently transferred to Calcutta and on a fortnight's break, had come to visit his sister tonight.

Everything took on a festive air for about ten days. Before Bishwambhar left, he asked his sister about the boys' mental acumen and progress in studies. In reply he had an earful about how brash and disobedient Phatik was, and how docile and studious Makhan appeared beside him.

"Phatik is a nuisance," his mother complained, "He gives me no peace—what a pain in the neck!"

Hearing this, Bishwambhar proposed taking Phatik back to Calcutta with him and enrolling him in a good school there. It was easy for Phatik's mother to accept this proposal.

On a rare moment when Ma found Phatik alone, she asked him, "Oh, Phatik dear, want to go to Calcutta with Uncle?"

"Yes, Ma; oh yes, yes!" Phatik was all eagerness, so much so as to drive his uncle nearly crazy; "when, oh when are we to leave?" he asked over and over again. So excited was he that he could hardly sleep nights.

Phatik's mother had no qualms about her son's leaving her, especially as she was very afraid he might hurt Makhan physically; she even went as far as to imagine that he might try to drown Makhan. Even then, his seemingly excessive enthusiasm left her feeling dejected.

When at last it was time to go, Phatik in his joyous excitement was liberal enough to bequeath all his kites, tops, marbles, rod & reel and every other toy he had to Makhan and his descendants.

Upon arrival at Calcutta, the first person Phatik met was his aunt. Now, to be honest, I don't think Auntie was at all pleased at this unnecessary addition to her family. Here was she, mother, wife and established mistress of her own home with her three teen-aged boys; and there like an unpleasant revolution appeared this unfamiliar, illiterate rustic thirteen-year-old. Even at his age, Biswambhar sometimes acted so childish!

There seems to be no other such nuisance on the face of the earth as a thirteen- or fourteen-year-old. He is neither good-looking nor useful. He cannot be loved for his own sake, nor is his company pleasant. Lisping seems childish, and adult talk is precocity—in fact, all talk seems frivolous. He shoots up so suddenly that his clothes no longer fit, which is seen as forwardness. All his baby cuteness and sweetness of voice seem to go suddenly, for which people are quick to blame him in secret.

Many faults of childhood and early manhood may be easily overlooked, but in an adolescent even a small lapse looms large. He too realizes that in his new state of physical and mental upheaval he does not quite fit anywhere; as such he is often embarrassed and apologetic for his very existence, and craves acceptance and affection. If he finds love and affection in a certain person, he becomes that person's slave and shadow. No one, however, dares to show open affection to him for fear of being labeled a softie. So, no wonder he begins to look and act like a stray dog.

In such a situation, any other place but his mother's seems a hell on earth. At every step the unloving disregard stings him like poisoned barbs. Girls and women seem like goddesses or angels, so their neglect hurts all the more.

What injured Phatik most was that to his unloving aunt he seemed a thorn on her side. As a result, whenever she asked him to do anything, he would enthusiastically do much more than was asked for. Then his aunt would throw cold water on his enthusiasm and remind him that he needed to finish prep. At such times her apparent anxiety for him seemed a cruel taunt.

In addition to the loveless atmosphere at home, poor Phatik hadn't a moment to himself. Hemmed in by four prisonlike walls, he would remember the uncomplicated freedom of his village home nostalgically. The open field where he and his companions would fly their kites, the riverfront where he would roam humming a sometimes cacophonous melody, the tiny rivulet where he would splash in and swim to his heart's content any time of day, and above all that witch of a mother of his would flash in his mind's eye and seem to call him.

The tall, lanky, graceless youth was embarrassed at his inability to fit in; he was consumed by an ardent desire, a blind craving to go to his mother. Like a lost calf at sunset, a helpless cry of "Oh Ma!" seemed to wrench his whole being.

There never seemed to have been such a dunce at school. If the teacher asked him a question, he only stared blankly and was silent. Then, when the teacher began to cane him, he bore it all without flinching. At recess he stood at the clear-paned windows looking far out at the roofs of houses in the neighborhood; if a child or two came up to the roofs for a while his heart would yearn to go out to them.

Once, he had dared to ask Uncle, "Please Uncle, when can I go home to Ma?"

"Let the holidays begin," Uncle had replied, but it seemed eons indeed before October and the Puja holidays; and as if to add insult to injury, one day Phatik lost his English textbook. Studies never came to him easily, and losing his textbook only made him want to throw in the towel all the more. Every day the teacher caned and humiliated him in front of his classmates. Such was his position in school that his cousins were embarrassed to own relationship with him. When Phatik was punished they appeared more amused than anyone else—as if by force.

Unable to bear any more, Phatik faced his aunt one evening with the confession, "I've lost my English textbook."

Auntie curled up her lips, "Now isn't that great! I can't buy you a book every time you lose one!"

Phatik said no more and came away; the realization that he was being a frightful expense to his aunt and uncle made him upset at his mother, with his meanness and poverty heightening his unease.

Phatik came home that evening with a raging, throbbing headache; feeling cold, clammy and shivery, he realized that a fever was on its way and that his aunt would be very irritated if he got sick. That this inept, foolish lad would expect to be nursed to health by anyone except his mother seemed to be too embarrassing even to dream of.

The next morning, Phatik seemed to have disappeared without a trace. An extensive house-to-house search of the neighborhood proved fruitless.

It had been raining sheets and curtains since dusk the evening before, so that everyone who turned out to look for Phatik got soaked to the skin. Unable to find Phatik anywhere, his uncle called the police.

At day's end, a police van blowing its siren from time to time braked to a stop before Bishwambhar's house. It was still raining sporadically; the road in front of Bishwambhar's house was under knee-deep water.

Two police officers, a man and a woman, helped a wet, muddy, miserably shivering Phatik up the walk to his uncle's front door. Phatik's face was flushed and his eyes red and bleary. Mr. Bishwambhar almost carried him inside.

His aunt, who had been so agitated all day as not to have had a proper meal and scolded her own three boys needlessly, burst out on seeing him, "Why go to all this trouble for other people's child? Just send him home."

"I was on my way home to Ma," wailed Phatik, hot tears spilling from his eyes, "But they brought me back."

All that night, Phatik was very ill with a high, delirious fever. Mr. Bishwambhar had to call the doctor.

Phatik opened his bleary, red eyes and stared dazedly at the door, asking, "Uncle, are the holidays here yet?"

Wiping his eyes on his handkerchief, Mr. Bishwambhar came to sit beside Phatik and took the child's thin hot hand affectionately in his.

Phatik mumbled deliriously, "Ma, please don't hit me; I haven't done any wrong."

Next day at daylight, Phatik opened his fever-bleared eyes and seemed to be looking for someone. Not finding whom he was looking for, he sighed and turned dispiritedly to face the wall.

Knowing and understanding just whom Phatik was seeking, his uncle leaned over to whisper in his ear, "Phatik my child, I've already sent for thy mother."

Another day passed; the doctor came and went with a grave face and could offer but little hope. Meanwhile Bishwambhar, with a rapidly sinking heart, waited for his sister and her younger son.

In his delirium, Phatik imitated the boatswains and chanted, "O . . . n . . . e fathom down . . . . , t . . . w . . . o fathoms down." On the way to Calcutta a year ago, he and his uncle had had to travel a leg of the journey by steamboat, where the boatswains would throw a thick sheet down into the water and melodiously fathom the depth of it. They could do this, but young Phatik could in no way fathom the depth of the eternal ocean which he would now have to cross.

The dusk had thickened when Phatik's mother, with little Makhan in tow, came in and started to weep and wail loudly while little Makhan stood by with a very scared face. When Bishwambhar had with great pains succeeded in calming her down, she threw herself down on her son's bed and cried, "Phatik, oh Phatik, my darling!"

"M . . . m," Phatik seemed to reply easily enough, "Ma dear, the holidays are here for me at last, and I'm going home."

8 THE MUTE
(ORIGINAL: SHUVA)

In Bengali, Shuvashini (Shuva) means a girl who speaks well. This story is Tagore's attempt to fathom the psychology of a mute maiden named Shuva. Because she cannot speak, everyone misunderstands Shuva.

WHEN SHUVASHINI WAS given that name, no one had any inkling that she would turn out to be mute. Her two elder sisters were named Sukeshini and Suhashini, so her father named his youngest daughter Shuvashini to rhyme her name with her sisters'. Now that name has been shortened to Shuva.

After some real and thorough investigation, the two elder girls were married; now only the youngest remained, as a silent burden to her parents.

Not everyone realizes that a mute person can feel. So nobody thought much about expressing anxiety about Shuva even in her presence. She was given to understand from a very early age that she was born as a curse to her parents. As a result, she always tried to hide from people, thinking, 'Just let everyone forget about me.' However, pain is not so easy to forget; like a rankling sore Shuva was always on her parents' mind.

Her mother thought of her as her own biggest mistake, especially as a mother regards daughters more part of herself than sons, and sees any shortcoming in them as embarrassing. Her father, rather, seemed to love her more. Her mother thought of her as an irritating nuisance.

Shuva had no words, but her very muteness spoke volumes through her big long-lashed black eyes, and deep feeling made her lips tremble like new leaves in the wind.

When we speak, we have to think about what we would say, rather like translating; it does not always come out right, and sometimes there are big mistakes. However, big black eyes haven't got to translate anything—the mind casts automatic shadows on them; expressions open and close on them; sometimes they sparkle brightly; at other times they are pale, dark and inscrutable; sometimes they dim like a setting moon, at other times brightening slowly like lightning flashing. For someone who has had nothing but the unspoken language of her eyes to express her feelings all her life, that depth of expression reaches to the bottom of the heart and is unendingly liberal—rather like a clear sky, with its inscrutable interplay of light and shade. This voiceless person has greatness not unlike that of open nature. Thus was it that she had no young playmates, for the other children were a bit afraid of her. She was as friendless and quiet as a desolate noontide.

The village was called Chandipur. The river beside her, more a stream than a real river, was like the girl next-door, not extending much farther than a mile or two, doing her work with a quiet unceasing murmur of companionship. It was as if she tied the villages on each of her banks with the silver thread of amity, fastened in a double square knot. On each bank were trees and homes. Below these the pretty little rivulet danced along, doing her good work, bringing benediction to everybody.

Banikantha's house was right on the edge of the riverbank. The signs of prosperity that set him apart from the rest of his neighbors was clearly visible in the well-built huts with fences all around them, the well-kept barn, the threshing-room, the hayricks, the two tamarind trees with the space below them swept clean, the little orchard with various species of mango trees and of jackfruit and banana trees catch the eye of every boatman and passenger traveling on the river. Among all these visible signs of comfort, the little mute lady managed to elude everyone's eye; whenever she could spare a moment or two, she would come sit on the riverbank.

It seemed that Mother Nature lovingly compensated her want of language by speaking for her. The murmurous flow of the river, the mingling of many voices in conversation, the slow songs of a boatman, the calling of all kinds of birds, the rustling of leaves in the trees—the mixing and merging of all these broke like waves at the silent heart of this slip of a girl. This was the unspoken language of the mute—just like the language of young Shuva's long-lashed dark eyes: the chirping of crickets, silent gestures and movements, music, tears and sighs.

When the boatmen and the fishermen went on their lunch break, the homeowners went to siesta, and even the birdcalls and the ferryboats paused, the peopled world suddenly fell silent as if devoid of all life, at that moment under the sunlit canopy of Heaven sat this mute maiden in communion with a world as silent as she herself, in the shade of overhanging trees.

It isn't as if Shuva had no close friends—the two young heifers in the barn, named Sarbashi and Panguli, though by this unspeaking damsel they'd never heard their names called, but they knew her and recognized her step; they also fathomed the thoughts that she never spoke, much easier than her speaking relatives did. They understood when Shuva was petting them, when she scolded them, and even, it seemed, when she was pleading with them.

Stepping into the barn, Shuva would hug Sarbashi and rub her cheeks near the heifer's soft floppy ears, while little Panguli would be close by, looking on and licking Shuva's face from time to time. The maiden would pay regular visits to the barn three times a day, apart from the numerous unscheduled calls upon her two animal friends. Whenever she had a bad day, she would console herself with a visit to Sarbashi and Panguli, and a hug for each of them. They seemed to know that she needed uncritical companionship at those times especially, and would try to make her feel better by nestling close and rubbing their horns on her in silent sympathy.

Apart from these there were kittens and a kid goat too. However, with these young Shuva had no close relationship. However, they too would show their obedience and docility in different ways. The little kitty would climb into Shuva's warm lap and go to sleep at all hours of the day, indicating by contented purrs that she enjoyed it when Shuva stroked her back.

Among higher beings too Shuva had a companion. However, just what her relationship to him was needed some clarification, because he could talk. So, at least linguistically, they were not equals.

He was the younger son of the Gonsais, named Pratap. He seemed to be a very indolent fellow. After trying their utmost to engage him in some useful profession, even his parents had given up on him. Relatives and friends are annoyed at lazy people, but strangers like them a lot. They have the distinct advantage of never being busy; they are readily available to run any errand, and become sort of common handymen. Just as there are public gardens and parks in the city, so should there be a few public odd job men who are there to do any little task that needs doing, especially at festivals, parties and funerals.

Pratap's main hobby was angling, an occupation which requires both time and patience. On many afternoons he could be seen casting his line into the water and waiting for the fish to bite. And on such occasions he often met Shuva. Whatever he was doing, Pratap would always feel better if he had someone to share it with. While one is fishing, a mute companion is the best. Pratap realized this, and as such he valued Shuva. Thus, while everyone else was content to call her Shuva, Pratap with a little more affection called her Sue.

Shuva would sit waiting under the tamarind tree, while not far away would be Pratap, casting his line into the water and waiting for the fish to bite. Pratap had a prepared paan due him, and Shuva would always prepare it herself with great care. Perhaps she felt the urge to be of use to him, to help him in some way, and to let him know that even mute Shuva had some worth on this earth, during those long, sometimes very boring hours of waiting. However, there was nothing to do. Then speechlessly she would pray to God to endow her with supernatural powers, so that she could do something unforeseen and magical, to attract his attention. Seeing that, perhaps Pratap would think, "Oh, look at that! I'd no idea our Subhi had such magical powers!"

Suppose Shuva were a mermaid, and she were to rise out of the sea to leave the jewel from the cobra's head on the step just above the water; Pratap would leave off his silly fishing to pick up that gem and dive underwater with it; and in Neptune's undersea palace, in her room on her gold bedstead would be . . . . who else but our mute Sue, Banikantha's little girl? Our little Sue would be the lone princess in that castle in the deep, lit only by the glow of the pearls shining through the water. Oh, could that never be? Was it so improbable? Nothing is that impossible, but even then Sue was born into Banikantha's house and not in an undersea kingdom devoid of subjects, and had nothing to astonish Pratap with.

Shuva was getting older by the day. As she grew physically, so did she begin to feel and know herself and the world around her. It was as if on a moonlit night a tide of new feelings flooded into her. She was observing herself pensively, questioning herself, and not getting a satisfactory answer.

Sometimes on late moonlit nights she would open her bedroom door and stick her face out to gaze timidly at the silent landscape, which awake and alone seemed to be guarding the sleeping world—in all the mystery, pleasure and melancholy to the outer limits of the solitary silence, unspeaking yet eloquent in its very muteness. At the very edge of all this silence stood a mute girl, eager yet unable to speak.

When he returned he urged, "Come, let us hie ourselves to Calcutta."

Arrangements for the trip abroad were afoot. Shuva's heart filled with tears, like the film of mist that shrouds the earth on a foggy morning. A vague apprehension made her stick close to her parents for a while, wanting to understand it all. Her unspoken message went west; never did they explain anything.

One afternoon in the meantime, Pratap cast his line into the water and said with a chuckle, "Hi, Sue, I hear they've found a bridegroom for thee and thou art to be married? See that thou forget us not."

So saying, he turned back to his fish. Just as a doe with an arrow through her heart looks mutely at her killer as if to say, 'How have I wronged you?' so did Shuva gaze at Pratap now; she did not wait under the tree that day. Instead, she went in to her father, where he sat smoking in the bedroom after his nap, sat at his feet looking up at his face and started to cry. Trying to console her, her father wept too and his tears fell thick and fast.

The next day, the family would leave for Calcutta. Shuva went to the barn to take leave of her childhood playmates, fed them with her own hands, hugged them and spoke to them mutely with those eloquent eyes of hers, her tears coursing down her cheeks.

It was the twelfth night of the lunar month. Shuva came out of her bedroom and walked to the riverbank where she lay down on the soft grass as if to hug the earth, this expansive mother of man, and say, 'Please Mother, don't let me go. Wrap thine arms about me as I have wrapped mine around thee and hold me to thyself.'

At an apartment in Calcutta one evening, Shuva's mother made her up fantastically. Her hair was done up tightly with gold ribbon wrapped around it, and she was covered with jewelery from head to toe so that her natural beauty was all but hidden. Shuva was in tears; her mother scolded her a lot lest her eyes swell up and she look bad in front of the bridegroom's party; however, her tears would not stop.

The prospective bridegroom himself came with a friend for the viewing of his future bride—her parents were anxious, fearful and flustered, as if the deity himself had appeared to choose the animal for a sacrifice. Mother screamed and scolded, so Shuva cried even more, and sent her to face her examiners. He observed her long and hard, concluding, "Not bad; not bad at all."

Especially when he saw her weeping he realized that she had a heart, and figured out, 'the heart which is saddened today at the thought of parting from her parents will serve me well later.' Like a pearl in its shell the maid's weeping only increased her worth, not saying anything more for her.

Matching up the horoscopes, the wedding took place in an auspicious moment.

Giving their mute daughter in marriage, the parents returned home and all was saved.

The bridegroom was employed out west. Soon after the wedding, he took his bride there.

Within a week everyone realized that the bride was mute. It wasn't her fault that no one found out until it was too late. She had cheated no one. Her eyes had told all; they had simply not understood. She looked around her, not finding words or the faces she had known since birth; an all pervading, unspoken cry seared her ever-silent heart that no one but God heard.

This time, after careful scrutiny, her husband married a girl who could see, hear and talk.

9
THE POSTMASTER
(ORIGINAL: POSTMASTER)

The central character in this story is based on a real postmaster. Tagore elaborates what may happen to a city-dweller suddenly sent to the countryside. The feeling of discomfiture, of being the odd person out, pervades the whole being. Even if a sweet relationship does form, it doesn't last. Such is the close, sweet relationship between the postmaster and Ratan, his servant-girl. In that situation, Ratan was the only person who could care for the postmaster. Yet, because Ratan was no blood kin, the postmaster had to sever all ties with her when he was transferred out.

AT THE OUTSET of his very first job, the postmaster had to move to the mean, small village of Ulapur. The European director of the nearby indigo-plantation had singlehandedly set up this small new post office.

Our postmaster was a city man, Calcutta-born and bred. This very remote outpost of civilization made him feel like a fish out of water. A dark bungalow shaded by leafy mango trees was his office; a pond of water hyacinths, thickly wooded on all sides, was close by. The petty clerks and other officials of the factory were either too busy or too indifferent to associate with gentlefolk.

A young man especially Calcutta-bred has no idea of how to mix freely with other people. In unfamiliar settings he is either painfully shy or brashly forward. Thus our postmaster found himself unable to make many friends among the local people. However, as his job demanded but little time and effort, he would compose poems during his long leisure hours, where he wrote that he passed his time very pleasantly indeed looking at the swaying leaves and clouds & listening to birdsongs—but God Almighty knows well, if some ogre of the Arabian Nights were to appear suddenly and clear away all these trees to build skyscrapers that obscure the sky, our half-dead city man would get a new lease on life.

Living off a very meager salary, our postmaster would shop and cook for himself. A teenage damsel from the nearby locality did his other chores for him, thus earning her bread. About fourteen years old, in appearance plain rather than pretty, and an orphan to boot, she was no prospective bride for anyone; her name was Ratan.

In the dusky evenings, when smoke curled from the barns in the village, crickets chirped shrilly from the hedges, and the lunatic drunks of the village broke into cacophonous song accompanied by clashing cymbals and beating drums—when his heart would tremble with the trembling of the leaves in the dark, he would light a dim lamp in the corner of the room and call, "Ratan! Oh Ratan dear, where art thou?" Ratan would be right at the door, awaiting this summons; but never would she hie herself there at once. Instead, she would ask back, "What is it, Sir? Why do you need me?"

"What art thou doing?" The postmaster would ask.

"I was on my way to the kitchen, to light the stove . . ."

"Oh, never mind the kitchen! Go get me my tobacco, now."

In just minutes, Ratan would appear with cheeks puffed up, hot and sweaty from blowing into the bell of the bubble pipe to keep the coals glowing. Taking it from her, the postmaster would ask suddenly, "Oh, Ratan dear, dost thou remember thy mother?" That was a very long story indeed; she remembered only bits and pieces of it. Her father, who had been a rickshaw-puller, had loved her more than her mother ever had. She remembered more of him than of her mother. After his day's work her father would come home to their little shanty, sometimes bringing treats, and Ratan & her little brother would vie for his attention. One or two of these happy evenings were etched clearly in her memory. These tales would sometimes proceed far into the night, and perhaps the Postmaster would feel too lazy to cook again; with leftover curries from the morning's meal and some chapattis which Ratan would hurriedly roll out and pan-fry, she and the Postmaster would have supper.

Some evenings, the Postmaster, sitting on his wooden stool in the big room which served as his office, would talk of his own family—of his younger brother, of his mother and elder sister—for whom his heart yearned, yet of whom he could talk to no one else; these tales he would tell with a perfectly straight face to this illiterate village maiden, with nothing seeming amiss. At last it became so that Ratan would mention his family as Ma, Didi or Dada, as if she had known them all the time. She had even imagined out in her little heart what they might look like.

One noontime during the Rains, the clouds had given way to a little sunshine, and a soft warm breeze blew. The sun heating up the wet grass smelt damp and breathy, as if the warm wet breath of the weary earth were touching one. A relentless mama bird sent up her unceasing plaintive call to the seemingly deaf ear of Mother Nature. The Postmaster was enjoying a leisurely afternoon, observing the rain-washed, silky soft leaves swaying and the mass of rain-clouds burning up in the sunshine. He was thinking he wanted someone he cared about to share this with him, someone he really loved very much. Gradually it began to seem as if the bird was calling out this alone, and that the inner significance of the trembling leaves on this quiet tree-shaded afternoon was something like this. No one seems to know or to want to believe, but these thoughts sometimes do assault the soul of a meagerly paid postmaster of a small village on a silent holiday noontide.

Sighing, the postmaster called, "Ratan! Oh Ratan dear, wherefore art thou?"

Ratan was right then sitting sprawled under the guava tree, eating green guavas. Hearing her master's voice she ran up at once panting, "Dadababu, did you want me?"

"I shall teach thee to read, bit by bit," said the Postmaster. The whole afternoon passed very quickly in lessons, and in a few weeks they were past their diphthongs.

In the month of Shravana there is no end to the rains. All ponds, streams and lakes, and of course the little river, swelled up and filled to the brim. The sound of torrents of rain was heard day and night, coupled with the croaking of every species of frog in the region. People needed boats to move about, even to go to market.

One day it had rained since early morning. The Postmaster's young student had waited a long while at her usual spot by the door.

However, not hearing the customary call, she willed herself to enter the room.

The Postmaster, she saw, was lying on his little pallet. Thinking he was resting, she turned to go, but couldn't—for suddenly she heard, "Ratan!"

The weak voice did not sound at all like the Postmaster's usual robust one. Turning quickly, Ratan asked, "Dadababu, were you calling me?"

In a very strained voice the Postmaster said, "I don't feel very well; please feel my forehead and see if I have a temperature."

In this very solitary exile on a very miserably rainy day such as this, a sick person craves attention, and likes to think that his mother and sister are with him, tending to his needs; here too the exile's wish came true. Ratan remained no longer a mere girl. From that moment she became as a mother. She fetched the apothecary, gave the patient his pills on time and stayed awake beside him all night, asking frequently, "Oh Dadababu, are you feeling a little better?"

After a long illness, the postmaster, thin and wan, quitted his sickbed. He made up his mind to seek a transfer by any means, and right away wrote a petition to the authorities in Calcutta seeking a transfer.

Relieved of nursing, Ratan resumed her usual post near the door. However, no regular call now came. Peeking in from time to time, she would see the Postmaster sitting distractedly on his pallet or lying down. Here sat Ratan, awaiting his call, while there was he, waiting eagerly for an answer to his petition. The little lady sat besides the door reading over her old lessons a hundred thousand times, lest she make a stupid mistake when at last the call did come. At last, about a week later, she was called in one evening. With a rapidly beating heart she entered, asking, "Did you send for me, Dadababu?"

"Yes, Ratan dear. I am leaving tomorrow," stated the postmaster.

"But where to, Dadababu?" She asked, bewildered.

"Home," replied he.

"When will you be back?"

"Never again," responded the Postmaster.

Ratan asked no more. The Postmaster told her himself that his application for a transfer had been turned down, so he had no other recourse but to quit his job. After this, nobody spoke for a very long time. The lamp flickered dimly, and rainwater dripped into an earthen dish through a hole on the roof.

A little later, Ratan got up slowly to go to the kitchen and roll out chapattis. She could not do this as quickly as she would have on other nights. Perhaps many confused thoughts crowded her young head. After the Postmaster finished his meal the girl asked, "Dadababu dear, can I come with you?"

"How on earth can that ever be?" laughed the Postmaster. He did not think it necessary to explain why this could not be to the lass.

All night, in sleep and waking, the Postmaster's laughing voice, "How on earth can that ever be?" Seemed to ring in Ratan's ears.

Rising in the early morning, the Postmaster found his bathwater ready as usual. According to his Calcutta custom, he would bathe in reserved water. For some reason, Ratan could not ask the Postmaster the night before when he'd be leaving. She had fetched his bathwater from the river late the night before anyway, in case he did need it. Ratan was summoned after the Postmaster had done bathing. Entering silently, Ratan looked up at her master as she awaited his command. The master said, "Ratan, I shall ask the gentleman who replaces me to care for thee just as I did. Thou hast not to worry because I'm leaving." No doubt these words were intended to be the kindest in the world, but who on the face of the earth understands a woman's heart? Ratan had on many previous occasions endured unflinchingly much sharper reprimands from her master, but these soft words made her burst into floods and floods of tears. Weeping hard she said brokenly, "No, no, you don't have to tell anybody anything. I will not stay."

The Postmaster had never seen Ratan behave like this before, so he was very surprised.

The new Postmaster arrived; handing the charges over to him, the former Postmaster prepared to depart. Calling Ratan to him he gave her all his salary except his traveling expenses in a white envelope, "Ratan, my dear girl, I wasn't able to pay thee before; now when I'm leaving, take this money. It will tide thee over the next week or so."

Falling on the dusty ground, Ratan clasped her master's feet, "Dadababu, I beg you, I implore you, you don't have to give me anything. I entreat you, no one has to worry about me—" and ran from the place as if a thousand devils were at her heels.

With a long, deep sigh, the former postmaster slung his umbrella over his shoulder and picked up his little carpetbag. Calling a porter to carry his blue and white tin box, he slowly walked towards the little boat tied to the riverbank.

When he was on the boat and it had started moving, with the rain-swollen river murmuring around it, he felt a twinge of nostalgia; the face and form of the young village maiden rose before him, making him hurt horribly. "What if I were to go back and take her with me? I'll do just that," he thought; by then the cremation-grounds at the very end of the village had come into sight and on the fast-flooding tide the sails had caught the wind. The river-farer thought disinterestedly, "What indeed is the use of going back? Who is whose, in this vast world?"

Young Ratan, however, had no such philosophy in mind as she circled the post-office in tears. Perhaps she hoped against hope that her beloved Dadababu might come back yet. It was that thought that did not let her go very far from the post-office. O, foolish, foolish human heart! Errors never cease, logic is comprehended only too late, false hope is clung to disregarding all proofs to the contrary until it too flees having drunk all one's life-blood; then one comes to one's senses and yearns for a second error to replace the first one.

10 THE SKELETON ON THE WALL (ORIGINAL: KANKAL)

This story is a figment of the imagination. Sometimes it is amusing to imagine what would transpire if inanimate objects had a voice of their own, and could tell their own story. This is just what Tagore does here.

THE BEDROOM WHERE we three childhood mates used to sleep had a whole human skeleton hanging on one wall. Its bones would rattle in the night air. During the day we had to handle those bones. At that time we used to study the Meghnad Badh with an old preceptor and anatomy from a graduate student of the Campbell School of Medicine. Our guardian wished us to be suddenly proficient in every subject; how far his wish has been granted, those who don't know needn't, and those who do better keep under wraps.

It has been quite a long while since then. The skeleton has gone from that room now, who knows where, and the same is true of the anatomy that we learned.

A few weeks ago, the house was so full that I had to bed down in that room at night. I couldn't sleep, because the bed was unfamiliar. While I tossed and turned, the church clock struck the hours one by one. In the meantime, the oil lamp that had been burning in the room went out too, after flickering dimmer and dimmer for about five minutes. There had been a few accidents at home ere this. So the idea of death was not so foreign; in fact, the just-extinguished flame reminded us forcefully of souls being called to the Lord, at all hours of the day or night.

Gradually the memory of that skeleton came into sharper and sharper focus in my mind. As I lay awake thinking of the time when it had lived, I felt something alive moving around and around my bed, groping about to find something, and breathing in short hard gasps as it moved. Failing to find what it sought, it spun around in ever-faster circles. I realized that I had fallen a prey to fancy, and that what sounded like footsteps was really my own blood pounding in my veins as it rushed to my head. Even so, I could not prevent a chilly shiver from running up and down my spine. Trying to force this apprehension out, I called aloud, "Who's there? Please answer." The footsteps halted near my mosquito-net and I heard an answer, "It's only me, come to find that skeleton of mine."

I thought, I shouldn't be afraid of my own fabrication; clutching the cushion so hard that my nails ripped holes in it, I remarked familiarly, "What a thing to do, now at midnight! So—o, what do you want that skeleton for, after all this time?"

In the dark, the response came from right beside my mosquito net, "O dear, what are you saying? That skeleton held my breastbones; all the youth and beauty of my twenty-six years of life blossomed around it. Now, would you think it odd that I want so much to see it just one more time?"

"That sounds logical enough," said I with a certain degree of flippancy, "So, please go looking and leave me alone to try and get some sleep."

Said she, with a hint of a smile in her voice, "You're alone, aren't you? Then let me sit here a while and talk like a human being. It's been thirty-five years since I sat in human company and talked. All these years since then I've been blowing like an ill wind over these cremation grounds. I'll sit here tonight and talk to you as a human being would."

I felt someone sit next to my mosquito net. Seeing no way out, I said with assumed cheerfulness, "Oh, all right; tell me a cheery story."

"If you want an amusing story," she said, "Allow me to tell you the story of my life."

The church clock struck two.

"When I was alive and young," my unseen visitor began, "I lived in deadly terror of one person—my husband. Around him, I felt just like a fish out of water, as if some unknown beast was trying to force me out of house and home—there seemed to be no stopping him. He was much older than I, and two months after our wedding he passed on. My relatives mourned long and hard on behalf of me. Matching numerous signs and symbols of the zodiac, my father-in-law said to my mother-in-law, "This girl is a demon in disguise." I remember that very clearly . . . hey, are you listening? How's this story?"

"Good," said I, "That is quite an amusing beginning for the story."

"Then listen. Happy and relieved, I came back to my father's house. I began to grow up, inside as well as outside. I knew that I was pretty. People would try to hide it from me, but I realized that a woman as beautiful as I was no easy person to find. What do you think?"

"Probably; but you see, I've never laid eyes on you."

"Oh, come on now! Why, you've seen that skeleton of mine, haven't you? Hee hee hee! I was just kidding. How can I prove to you, though, that two beautiful bright black eyes veiled by long black fans of lashes once inhabited those ugly gaping eyeholes, and that the unsightly grin that you now see on those bones is nothing compared to the sweet smile playing on two soft petal-pink lips? I am amused and irritated at once as I remember the blooming fullness and ripening youth that covered those long dry bones. Even the renowned physicians of that day did not seem to believe that anatomy students could use my body as a sample. I know that a certain student doctor described me to his special friend as a golden magnolia. Now tell me, has a magnolia any skeleton?"

"I realized that just as a diamond flashes fire when moved, so also did I radiate natural beauty with every step I took. I would often stretch my arms out in front of me and evaluate them as critically as I could—such arms as could have made snaring a man a piece of cake. When the beautiful Aphrodite drove her chariot across the heavens with Hephaestus beside her, she must have had such slim, fair, rounded arms, petal-soft, pink hands and well-shaped fingers with superbly manicured nails."

"However, that brazen, naked, stark and pitifully ancient skeleton of mine appears to have provided false testimony. There was no recourse for me then but to be silent. As such I am angrier with you than at any other person upon the face of this earth. O, how I wish you could see me at sixteen, so glowingly beautiful and vivacious! If you did, I swear your anatomy lessons would flee and you couldn't go to sleep."

Said I, "If you had a body, I'd swear by it that I've no whit of anatomy in my head. You at sixteen, so radiantly beautiful that it's difficult to look at you for very long, are in my mind's eye this very minute, fairer still because of the dark backdrop of night; you've to say but little more."

"Since Dada had vowed to remain a bachelor, I had no female relative or friend indoors. Sitting by myself under the flowering camellia tree in the garden, I'd imagine that the whole world was in love with me, that all the stars and planets were looking down at me and me alone from on high, that the wind was stroking my hair as it sighed coquettishly by again and again, and that if the grass seat I sat on with my legs spread out in front of me were conscious, it would swoon again at my touch. I imagined those grasses as all the young men who wanted to have a relationship with me, and somehow a twinge of vague pain tugged at my heart."

"When Dada's friend Sashisekhar (Sashi) graduated from medical school, he became our family physician. I had seen him many times before from a distance. Dada, I must add, was a very peculiar person; he seemed hardly aware of what went on around him. It was as if the world weren't big enough for him and he had kept moving over until he was cornered."

"Sashi, it seemed, was the only friend he had outside the family circle. As such, Sashi would often come over to the house and I would run into him; when at dusk I went to my grassy throne under the flowering tree, all the eligible bachelors of the world would congregate at my feet as Sashi, waiting silently for me . . . . Listening? How's the story?"

"Oh, if only I were Sashi!" I sighed.

"Listen to it all first . . . . One rainy day I woke up feeling feverish; the doctor came to see me. That was the first meeting.

"I lay facing the window, so the sick pallor of my face would be masked by the glow of the setting sun. When the doctor, upon entering, looked once at my face, I imagined myself in his shoes and looked down too, at a wan, flower-like face upon the soft pillow in the gathering dusk. A few loose curls lay in becoming disarray upon the pale forehead, and the long, fanlike lashes of downcast eyes shaded the flushed cheeks.

The doctor spoke softly to Dada, "I have to feel her pulse, please."

I got out my weary, rounded arm from under the covers; looking closely at it, I felt that it would have been much prettier had I worn some blue glass bangles. Really, I'd never seen a doctor hesitate so in feeling a patient's pulse—I could feel his fingers shaking. Don't believe me?"

"After a few more episodes of illness and recovery, I saw my evening meets reduced to just two participants—Sashi and me. It seemed that only a doctor and his patient were left upon the face of this earth.

"I'd secretly dress in a marigold-orange sari at eventide, put my hair up elegantly, wind a double string of jasmines around it and with mirror in hand, go sit on my grassy garden-throne.

"But why, oh, why ever on earth? Did looking at myself by myself no longer satisfy and please me? It really didn't, because no longer did I look at myself alone: I became two people. I'd observe and scrutinize myself, as a doctor would, be smitten and fall in love; I'd caress myself, but a sigh would rustle like the evening breeze at my heart.

From then on, I fancied myself alone no longer. When I walked, I would look down at my toes to see how they were touching the ground, and try to imagine how these footsteps affected our newly graduated doctor. The midday sun beat down mercilessly on the land; no sound save those of a few weary vendors vending their wares, or the almost inaudible swishes of kites' wings as they circled far overhead, could be heard. Spreading out a clean sheet under the tree, I'd lie down; resting a bare arm somewhat negligently on that soft bed, I would imagine someone approaching stealthily, picking up that petal-pink hand and gently kissing it before letting it go. Suppose the story were to end here. How about it, uh?"

"Not bad. Although it would be incomplete, I could pass the night pleasantly and busily enough trying to imagine the rest," said I.

"But . . . . But then the story would become all too serious; where would the ridicule be, and how would the skeleton beneath show itself in all its boniness?"

"Then listen; as Sashi's practice picked up, bit by little bit, he set up office in the ground floor of our house. As we got more and more familiar, I'd ask him laughingly about medicines and poisons, and how to die easily, and such stuff. Speaking of medicine, the doctor would open up. After repeated references, death became as familiar as a relative to me. I saw only love and death—and nothing else—upon the face of this earth."

"My story is nearly done; there is but little left to tell."

"So also has the night nearly passed," I said softly.

"For some time, I'd watched the doctor get more and more absent-minded and ill-at-ease, especially towards me. One evening I saw him borrow the horse-and-cart from Dada, to make a special trip. He had dressed with especial care."

"This was altogether too much for me to take. Going over to where Dada sat looking over some family accounts, I asked, among other things, "Oh Dada, where is the doctor off to tonight with the horse and cart?"

"'To die,' replied Dada tersely.

'No, no, please tell me the truth,' I pleaded, almost in tears.

Elaborating a little, Dada announced, 'To tie the knot.'

"'Oh, so that's it, is it?' I said, and burst out laughing as if I were going mad."

"By careful and gradual prodding I found out that the doctor would get twelve thousand Taka as dowry from this marriage. Why hide that fact, though, and plunge me into this humiliation? Had I told him that I would die of a broken heart if something of that sort happened? Men are never to be trusted. I've seen one man, and that's been enough for me to know all.

"When the doctor came in from seeing patients, just before dusk, I began to laugh a lot and asked, 'Hi, Doc, I hear you're to be married tonight?"

"My gaiety put the doctor ill at his ease, and he was downcast too.

"'What, no music?' I persisted.

"'Is a wedding an affair so joyous?' countered the doctor, sighing a small sigh.

"That made me laugh out; I'd never heard something so ridiculous. Said I,

'No way, not by a long shot; we must have lights, and music too.'

"I agitated Dada so much that he began then and there to prepare for a grand celebration.

I kept on and on, talking about what I'd do when the bride came home, and what might happen afterwards. 'Oh, I say, Doc,' I remarked as if I'd just thought of it, 'Would you still be seeing patients?'

"Hee, Hee! No one can read minds, especially a man's, but I'd swear by your body if I could that my words were hitting the doctor like poisoned darts.

"The wedding was scheduled for later that night. At dusk, the doctor sat having a glass or two of wine with Dada up on the roof; both had nurtured this little habit up to a level of fine dining. Slowly the dark sky lightened as the full moon rose.

I came forth laughing, 'Oh, Doc, have you forgotten? It's time to go.'

Here I must reveal a little detail. In the meantime, I'd secretly gone to the doctor's office and picked up some powder, which I had conveniently and discreetly mixed into his glass. I'd learned from the doctor himself what powders and how much were lethal.

Finishing his drink in one draught, the doctor said somewhat drowsily, 'I've got to go now,' and glanced a mortal glance at me.

"The flutes went on playing as I went up to my room and put on a gold-embroidered scarlet Vanarasi sari, every item of jewelry I owned out of the double locked safe, and a prominent streak of vermilion on the center part of my head. Then I spread the bed under my flowering camellia tree.

"It was a beautiful night. The full summer moon shed her silver radiance over the landscape, and a fair breeze blew cool over the sleeping city. The fragrance of just-blossomed jasmines was spreading out over the garden.

When the sound of the flutes grew faint in the distance, the moonlight darkened and this everyday world of ours faded dimmer and dimmer still in front of my eyes, I closed them and smiled.

"I had wanted people to see me with that beautiful smile on my lips like a colorful fantasy; I had wished that smile to go with me to my eternal bridal bower with Death. But alas! Where was the nuptial couch or indeed the wedding finery I had put on so carefully? Hearing a rattle within me, I woke up to find three young men taking anatomy lessons from their tutor with me as the model. Pointing at the place where the feelings had beat in the breast, and where my youth and beauty had unfolded like rose-petals, the tutor was telling them the names of the various bones. And, did you see any trace of that last smile on my lips?

"How was the story?"

"It was on the whole rather pleasant," I replied.

At that very moment the cock crowed and the eastern heavens blushed.

"Are you still there?" I asked. Only silence answered me as the sunlight flooded into the room.

11 THE WITNESS (ORIGINAL: RAMKANAIER NIRBUDDHITA)

This story shows us how greed can unravel the threads of family life. Here, Tagore has taken a situation that arises when a person dies intestate, and mixed the comic with the serious to show what can happen when a situation gets out of hand.

THOSE WHO SAY that while Gurucharan lay dying his second wife was playing cards make mountains out of molehills. The real story was that she was sitting on one leg with her other knee drawn up to her chin enjoying a bowl of watered rice with green tamarind, green chilies, and a very spicy dry curry of shrimp and spinach. When she was called out, she put aside her plate with its pile of chewed spinach stems and said in irritation, "There it comes again! I can't even have enough time to eat a little watered rice. What a life, indeed!"

In the meantime, when the doctor had said that Gurucharan had only a short while more to live, Gurucharan's younger brother Ramkanai sat down close to the patient and said slowly, "Dada, if you want to make a will, tell me now."

"Alright, take down what I dictate," said Gurucharan; Ramkanai brought out pen and paper. Gurucharan dictated, "I, Gurucharan, being of sound mind, hereby bequeath all my movable and immovable property to my wife, Baradasundari." Ramkanai wrote, but his pen moved slowly and unwillingly. He had hoped that his own only son, Navadwip, would inherit the property from Gurucharan, who was childless. Even if these two brothers lived separately, the hope of this inheritance had exhorted Navadwip's mother never to let her son find a source of steady income. She had also married him off early, and by God's grace he had one child already with another on the way. Even then Ramkanai wrote, and placed the will in front of Gurucharan for a signature. It came out as some crooked lines, which it would be almost impossible to decipher.

When his wife had finished eating and come out, Gurucharan's speech had stopped forever and she started to cry. "Crocodile tears," said those who had hoped to inherit but hadn't; however, that is surely not credible.

Hearing of what the will said, Navadwip's mother came up and made a ruckus fit to wake the dead; said she, "At the time of death, a man loses his wits. When there is such an eligible nephew around . . . ."

While Ramkanai revered his wife a lot, so much so that it may have been mistaken for fear, he could no more take this than he could a physical beating; said he, running up, "Mejobou, you haven't lost your wits too? You shouldn't behave like this now. Dada is gone, dear, but I'm still here. You can tell me what you need to later, when there's more time."

When Navadwip received the news and arrived, his uncle had passed on. Threatening the dead, he said, "I'll see who sets fire to your face; and if I hold a wake for you, my name isn't Navadwip." Gurucharan was a fellow who did not observe strict religious codes. He was a disciple of Dr. Duff. He would lean farthest towards the food that was taboo for him; in other matters too he liked to throw the Scriptures west. If people called him a Christian he would bite his tongue and say, "O Lord, may I eat beef if I'm a Christian." If such was the state of affairs while he was alive, it is doubtful he would mind not receiving due respect after death. However, on the face of it, this was the only way of retaliating. Navadwip consoled himself with the idea that his uncle would die in the afterlife. While he lived on this earth, he could make do without his uncle's property; but where his uncle had gone now he couldn't get his due by begging. There were distinct advantages to living.

Going up to Baradasundari, Ramkanai said, "Bouthakurani, Dada left all his property to you. Here is his will; put it away carefully in the iron safe."

The widow was right then making up stanzas in the melodious dirge she was engaged in, with her maidservants adding a verse or two here and there, causing a sleepless night for the village folk. The intrusion of this piece of paper in the midst of all this caused the rhythm to break off and the words went askew, too, so that it sounded sort of like this:

"Oh, what a thing to happen to me, how awful! Oh, Thakurpo, is this handwriting yours? Ah, my dear love, who will look after me now that you're gone? Who will take care of me?—stop, you all, don't scream and cry so much; let me listen. Oh, dearly beloved, why did I have to stay alive and not die sooner?" "That's just a stroke of ill luck for the rest of us," thought Ramkanai bitterly with a deep sigh.

When they arrived at home, Navadwip's mother flew aggressively at Ramkanai. Just like the patient ox that falls into a rut with a full cart and then has to tolerate the beatings of an irate driver motionlessly, Ramkanai had to endure the sting of her cutting words; then he just said simply, "I'm not at fault here. I'm no dada, for sure."

"No, you are so good," hissed Navadwip's mother sarcastically, "That you don't understand a thing. When Dada said, 'Take down,' the brother obediently wrote what was being dictated without a second thought. You are all the same. In due time you too are waiting to bring a scar-faced witch to this house, and disinherit my beloved Navadwip. But don't you worry, I am not so frail as to die as soon as all that."

Elaborating thus on Ramkanai's tortured future, his wife kept becoming more and more impatient. However, Ramkanai knew with unerring certainty that if he uttered even one word trying to dispel these acrid, irrational and unfounded, in fact imaginary, fears of hers, it would turn against him; so a wise apprehension made him hold his tongue, as if the undesirable deed of disinheriting darling Navadwip had already been done and he had nothing to do but confess.

In the meantime Navadwip, with the counsel of some clever friends, came and told his mother, "Please don't worry. I shall inherit. But first we have to get Papa out of here for a while. If he stays, he'll spoil everything. Navadwip's mother didn't trust her husband's intelligence one bit. So it is no wonder at all that the logic behind this suggestion seemed sound to her. So she drove her totally unnecessary, foolish spoiler of a husband to Kashi on some flimsy pretext.

In a few days, Baradasundari and Navadwipchandra took each other to court on charges of forging the will. From the will that Navadwip had turned in under his own name, the signature and handwriting clearly proved to be Gurucharan's; some selfless witnesses also turned up. On Baradasundari's side, Ramkanai, Navadwip's father, was the sole witness and the signature on the will was illegible; her cousin, who lived with the family, assured her, "Don't worry, Didi. I'll testify and also find more witnesses."

When the matter had progressed too long to turn back, Navadwip's mother recalled her husband from Kashi. That submissive gentleman returned just in time, canvas bag and umbrella in hand. He even tried to joke, going so far as to say with palms together, "Your Majesty, your faithful servant is here. Your wish is my command."

Shaking her head, the wife said, "Go on with you now! You don't have to joke and make fun. You were away from home so long on that flimsy pretext you didn't remember to contact me even once," etc.

Thus did the two parties thrust and parry loving complaints for quite a while—even going so far as racial slurs—until at last Navadwip's mother compared man's love to a Muslim's affection for a chicken or a duck.

"This woman has an iron hand in a velvet glove," thought Ramkanai, though when if ever that velvet glove had been revealed is a mystery.

In the meantime Ramkanai received a subpoena to appear in court as a witness. While he was in a bit of a muddle trying to figure it all out, Navadwip's mother appeared her eyes red with weeping. Seeing her husband she burst into floods and floods of tears, saying, "That irritating witch will not only send sweet Navadwip to jail, but she will also deprive him of his uncle's inheritance!"

Gradually grasping the whole matter, Ramkanai felt his world slowly black out before him. In a loud, trembling voice he screamed, "O dear Lord, what have you all done!"

Showing herself in her true colors at last, the wife bellowed, "What fault is it of Navadwip's? Would he let his uncle's inheritance go, just like that at the snap of a finger?"

What dutiful son of a good family can bear it when an unscrupulous, mercenary stranger comes to lay claim on what he believes to be his own? Even if at his deathbed a witch prompts a muddled, senile uncle to forsake his senses and the good nephew appears shortly afterwards to rectify the error by himself, what is wrong with it?

104

When the stupefied Ramkanai saw his wife and son shout, scream and shed tears alternately, he slapped his forehead hard and sat dumfounded, neither eating nor drinking.

Two days passed thus in silent inanition and then it was trial day. Meanwhile Navadwip had so coerced and bribed that cousin of Baradasundari's that he easily went over to Navadwip's side, testifying against Baradasundari. When Jayshree was preparing to go over to Navadwip's side, Ramkanai was called to the stand.

The parched-tongued, chapped-lipped old man, famished and nearly dead from hunger, got tremblingly up on the stand and clutched at it with fleshless, emaciated fingers. The witty barrister employed a slow, roundabout method of getting at the facts—starting from a long way off, he slowly inched closer and closer.

Then Ramkanai faced the judge and palms together, said, "Your Honor, I'm a very weak old man, unable to say much. Please let me be very to the point and concise in what I have to say. My elder brother the late Gurucharan Chakravarti bequeathed all his property to his wife Mrs. Baradasundari in a will before he died. I wrote that will myself, and Dada himself signed it. The will that my son Navadwichandra has presented is a fake." So saying, Ramkanai fell onto the floor of the stand in a shivering swoon.

The clever barrister said humorously to the attorney beside him, "By Jove! How we had the old man in our clutches!"

The cousin ran to Navadwip's mother saying, "The old man nearly spoilt it all. My testimony saved the day."

"My good Lord! I'd taken the old man to be a simple, good soul," wondered the sister, "Who can say what lies buried in man's heart?"

The friends and companions of the imprisoned Navadwip decided that the old man had done this because he had been scared witless in the witness box. Such a complete fool was scarcely to be found elsewhere in the city.

Returning home, Ramkanai fell ill with a high delirious fever. Repeating his son's name over and over in delirium this foolish, worthless man, this unnecessary father of Navadwip's who spoilt whatever he tried to do, left this world. Some relatives remarked, "He should have gone a few days earlier," but I don't want to mention their names.

12 TRUE RELIGION (ORIGINAL: MUSSALMANIR GOLPO)

This story teaches us that humanity transcends race, caste and creed. When someone is in danger and needs help, as a human being he or she is entitled to it. Any society that denies this is missing a vital link.

IT WAS A time when anarchists laid the rule of law waste, and every day and night would be swinging in the waves of this misrule. Daily living had become so nightmarish that people looked to the deities for salvation. Even then the fear of an evil eye kept everyone in tenterhooks. It was difficult indeed to trust anyone, be he man, or indeed, deity. Only the oath of tearful eyes was paid any attention to. There was little difference in the result of good or evil doings. Man would stumble often on his way to his allotted tasks.

At such a time, the birth or advent of a beautiful girl in any home was looked upon as a curse. If such a girl were born, her relatives would say, "We'll be relieved when this burnt-faced one goes away." Just such a problem had come to Bangshibadan, the owner of the only three-story home in the area.

Kamala was a comely maiden; her parents had passed on. If she too had gone with them, everyone would have been relieved. But that didn't happen, so her uncle Bangshi had brought her up very lovingly and carefully.

Her aunt, however, would often complain to neighbor women, "See, sisters dear, her parents left her with us only to our ruin. Who knows what trouble may beset us? I have children of my own; and here she is like a torch of annihilation—bad people are eying us from everywhere. I can't sleep for the fear that one day she alone will pull us under."

Days were going by just so; now a young man proposed to take her hand in marriage. In that fest, Kamala could never be hidden away. Her uncle would say, "That's why I'm looking for a young man who can keep her safe and sound."

The young man was the second son of Paramananda Seth, from Mochakhali. They were very wealthy, but once the father passed on, that'd probably vanish into thin air. The man was very foppish—he'd fly hawks, gamble, or put on a nightingale fight with great bravado, just to spend money. He was very vain of all that wealth of his, all his stuff. He had fat Bhojpuri strongmen to serve him, all famed as pole-wielders. He went around saying that there was no one born of woman who could hurt a hair on his head. He was quite a bit vain about women—he had one wife, and was looking for a second, younger one. He heard of the lovely Kamala. The House of Seth was as wealthy as it was powerful. They vowed to take Kamala as a bride.

"Kakamoni, where are you setting me adrift?" Wept Kamala.

"If I was able to keep you safe, my sweetheart, I'd have held you at my heart always, you know that," replied her uncle, miserably.

On the wedding day, the bridegroom came proudly to the assembly, with no end of music, fireworks and other ingredients for a grand party. The uncle folded his hands in supplication, "My boy, you shouldn't make such a to-do. Times are bad."

Hearing this, the young men swore, "We'll just see how they can come near us."

His Bhojpuri attendants twirled their mustaches and stood up, sticks in hand.

The young bridegroom was taking his bride home through the famed field of Taltardi. Madhumollar, the chief of a gang of highwaymen, fell upon the wedding party at second watch that night, with all his ruffians, lights blazing, roaring out like lions. Almost all the Bhojpuri attendants perished. Madhumollar was a notorious robber, from whose clutches few had escaped unscathed.

Fearfully, Kamala had climbed out of the sedan chair and was about to hide in some thick bushes; all at once, old Habir Khan, whom everyone respected almost as much as they do the Prophet (PBUH), materialized behind her. Standing tall and proud, he declared,

"Take off, sonnies! I'm Habir Khan."

"Khan Sahib," said one of the robbers, "We can't go against you. But why did you throw such a wrench in our business?"

Anyway, let go and take off they had to.

Coming up to Kamala, Habir said lovingly, "You're my daughter. Come with me to my house, my girl, out of this predicament."

Kamala seemed to shrink into herself.

"I understand. You're a Hindu Brahmin woman, shy of going into a Muslim home," said Habir Khan, "But I want you to remember one thing, dear. True Muslims respect religious-minded Hindus, too. In my house you'll live as a Hindu woman would; so come, my child. My home is close by. Let's go; I'll keep you very safe."

Kamala was a Brahmin woman, so her shyness was a long time breaking. Seeing this, Habir Khan spoke again, "Look, dear, there's no one in these parts who would lay a hand on your religion as long as I'm alive. Come you with me, don't be afraid."

Old Habir Khan took Kamala home. What a surprise, to see a temple to Shiva on one of the eight buildings of his compound, along with other accessories needed for Hindu religious rites!

An old Brahmin priest came, saying, "My dear, this place is just like a Hindu home. Here you can never be defiled."

"Please send word to my uncle. He'll come take me home," wept Kamala.

"My little girl, you're wrong. No one in that house will take you back now. If you don't believe me, go yourself and see," said Habir.

Habir Khan himself escorted Kamala to the back door of her uncle's house; said he, "I'll wait right here."

Going into the house, Kamala hugged her uncle by the neck, "Kakamoni, please don't let me go."

Her uncle's eyes brimmed with tears and spilled over. Her aunt, however, saw her and began screaming, "There's the spoiler, back from the house of another race! Push the poltergeist out, drive her away! Herald of ills, hast thou no shame coming back from a home with no caste?"

"There's no way, baby! We are a Hindu home; no one will take you back here. Moreover, we'd lose our caste, too," said her uncle.

Kamala stood there a while with her head down. Then slowly she crossed the outer threshold with Habir. Her uncle's door closed behind her forever.

In Habir Khan's home, Kamala had everything she needed and wanted to keep practicing her faith. Said he, "No son of mine will ever come to your quarters. This old Brahmin will help you with your worship and other Hindu rites."

This part of the house had a bit of history. This building was called the Rajputani Palace. An ancient Nawab had brought a Rajput lady there, keeping her apart from all the other women and thus preserving her chastity. She worshipped Shiva, occasionally going on pilgrimages, too. Noble Muslims of those days respected noble and religious-minded Hindus. There were many Hindu women that lady sheltered in this building, so they could observe and keep their faith. It was noised abroad that this man, Habir Khan, was that lady's son. He did not take his mother's faith, yet he did revere her in his heart. That mother is now no more, but to keep her memory fresh and to respect her, Habir Khan had taken on the especial vocation of saving these Hindu women who were molested in any way.

What poor Kamala got from them she'd never had in her uncle's house. Her aunt would often shove her aside, berate her as an unlucky omen, bringer of bad luck etc. and that the family line would be saved if she met death. Her uncle would sometimes buy her clothes or other things, always in secret, because her aunt would not approve. In this building that had once housed the Rajput lady, Kamala became as a queen. Here, she was enveloped in love and care; all the servants and maids she had were Hindu.

At last, Kamala attained the fullness of puberty. A young man of the home secretly began coming to her quarters, with whom she gradually fell in love.

It was then that one day she told Habir Khan, "Baba, I have no religion. The fortunate man whom I love is my creed. I do not see God's happiness in the faith which has kept me from love all my life, has flung me into the trash heap, so to speak. Father, here in this home of yours I first felt loved, knew that the life of a wretched woman like me has value, too. I worship the God who has sheltered me through this love . . . He is neither Muslim nor Hindu. I have taken Karim, your second son, to be my soul mate. My worship is tied up in him. Convert me to Islam, I won't object. What if do have two faiths?"

Thus did the story of their lives intertwine and proceed; there was no way for Kamala to meet her former relatives again. In the meantime Habir Khan made arrangements to make Kamala forget that she had been no relation. She converted, taking the name Meherjan.

In the meantime came the wedding of her uncle's second daughter. The arrangements were all as before, and the same predicament befell this party, too. The highwaymen swooped roaring down again. Their prey had slipped by them once. They weren't about to let that happen again, and were thirsting for revenge.

"Never! I forbid this!" came an answering roar from right behind.

"Oh no, here are Habir Khan's henchmen, to spoil everything"

When the bride's party wanted to run wherever they could, leaving the bride in her sedan chair, there, in their midst appeared the half-moon standard of Habir Khan, on the point of a lance. A stately lady bore it aloft, fearlessly.

She spoke to Sarala, "Have no fear, my dear sister. For thee I have the haven of Him Who turns no one away, never asking what caste or creed they are.—Kakamoni, my regards to you. Don't be afraid. I shan't touch your feet. Now take this dear girl back to your home; nothing and no one has sullied her. Tell Auntie I had to partake of her upbringing when she was unwilling, for a very long time indeed. I had no idea I could pay her back this way. I've brought a red wedding sari for my sister; here it is, and also an ivory cushion. If my sister is ever in trouble or pains again, all she has to remember is that she has a Muslim sister who will try her utmost to save her."

THE END

BIOGRAPHY OF THE TRANSLATOR

YASMIN FARUQUE WAS born on Nov. 11, 1955, in Dhaka, Bangladesh. She attended Viqarun Nisa Noon Girls' High School, Holy Cross College and the School of English Literature at Dhaka University. She has written stories and poems since she was a mere child. The present work, Tribute to Tagore, is her second attempt at translation. Her first, Moni Monjusha, a Bangla translation of short English poems, appeared in print in November 1979. Now married and the mother of an adult son, she lives in Grand Forks, ND, USA. Since 2005, she has presented stories, poems and essays at the Annual Writers' Conference at the University of North Dakota, Grand Forks. Eight of her book reviews were published in the Grand Forks Herald during 2005 and 2006.